AMISH JOY
BOOK 4 THE AMISH BONNET SISTERS

SAMANTHA PRICE

Copyright © 2019 by Samantha Price

All rights reserved.

No part of this book may be reproduced in any form or by any electronic or mechanical means, including information storage and retrieval systems, without written permission from the author, except for the use of brief quotations in a book review.

Scripture quotations from The Authorized (King James) Version. Rights in the Authorized Version in the United Kingdom are vested in the Crown. Reproduced by permission of the Crown's patentee, Cambridge University Press.

CHAPTER 1

It was now weeks after Florence's special encounter with Carter Braithwaite. When Florence woke, she nestled her head into her pillow, reliving the moments they'd shared. Helpless to prevent the secret smile that rested on her lips, she pulled the quilt higher until it covered her head in darkness.

Sleep had been elusive every night since the delightful kiss that had replayed in her mind no less than one thousand times.

One day he'd come to the community and want to join them. It wasn't likely, but she could still hope and dream. If it wasn't meant to happen, why had he been placed in front of her?

Now the biggest question was, if *Gott* wanted her to marry an Amish man, then, where was he?

Her mind had been continuously tormented by the questions that arose from her attraction to Carter.

She didn't feel guilty about sharing that kiss with him—she just didn't.

It had been the most wonderful, beautiful thing in the world.

Now she knew how *wunderbaar* life could be.

Her heart welled with happiness, so much happiness that she wanted to tell someone, but who would understand? Not her best friend, and not any of her family.

No one knew about her secret attraction to their neighbor, Carter Braithwaite. All they knew of him was that he lived next door and that he'd driven her to collect her half-sister, Honor, when she'd foolishly run away with Jonathon.

Her stepmother, Wilma, had thought nothing of his kindness. To her, it was reasonable that their neighbor would help them out in a crisis since they had urgently needed a car and a driver.

When they'd kissed, Carter had asked her, almost begged her, to visit him the next day, but in the early hours of the following morning her common sense had kicked in and she'd decided against it.

Since that kiss, Christmastime had come and gone, and now it was a mid-January morning.

Even though fear of the unknown had kept her away from him, that didn't stop her thinking about him every single minute. Part of her hoped he'd knock on her front door and say he couldn't live through another day without her.

What would she possibly say to him when she saw him again?

What would he expect?

How was she supposed to act?

It was better to stay away, if she could, for as long as she could. That was what she'd decided, but now —weeks along—her resolve was weakening.

She raised her hand, grabbed hold of the hand-stitched quilt and flung it off her. Then she stretched her arms above her head, letting out a long, sleep-deprived yawn. It was barely light outside. Pre-dawn was the best time for her to grab some peace before her noisy, half-sisters woke.

After exchanging her nightdress for her day dress, she pulled on her black stockings, apron and cape, and then sat down on the end of her bed. Pulling her loosely braided, thigh-length hair over one shoulder, she undid the braid, and slowly began brushing. Then she sectioned, braided, and pinned her hair up before donning her prayer *kapp* and getting to her feet.

As she walked down the stairs with her shoes in her hand for quiet's sake, she thought back to the letter she found in the attic—the one her mother had written to her. Her mother had told her not to make the same mistakes that she had made, but what had she meant by that?

Exactly what had her mother been trying to tell her, and why hadn't she made it clearer?

She'd always assumed her mother and father had been in love, but what if they hadn't been?

Even though it wouldn't change anything ... somehow, it would.

Then there was the other letter she'd found, the one written *to* her mother from a man named Gerald Braithwaite. He had begged her mother not to marry her father, and to leave the Amish to be with him.

Was history trying to repeat itself, with her now being tempted by a Braithwaite, who was also an outsider?

Carter had claimed to know nothing about a man by the name of Gerald Braithwaite. But to Florence, it had seemed more than a coincidence.

Florence walked into the quiet kitchen and slowly pushed up the blind to let in the winter-morning's

AMISH JOY

light. Then she filled the teakettle with fresh water and placed it on the stovetop.

Once she was sitting down at the kitchen table, she set about figuring how to find out about Eleanor—her mother's name. She knew none of her mother's relatives. The only cousins, aunts and *onkels* were those of her father's family—or her stepmother's family, and those weren't even blood-relatives to her.

No one ever talked about Eleanor. Even Florence's two older brothers had never mentioned anything about the mother the three of them had shared.

Florence decided all that was going to change. Today!

Since Earl was living in Ohio, Mark was the obvious choice of brother to speak with. She'd visit his saddlery store and ask him questions. It was easier to talk with him at work without his wife, around. Christina would have something to say. She always had something sour to say about everything. The rare occasions she kept her mouth closed, her looks said everything anyway.

Florence managed one cup of coffee before she was intruded upon by the girls and *Mamm*.

The Baker family no longer had the market stall

because they didn't have enough people to run it, and *Mamm* didn't want to employ anyone outside of the family. That meant that the not-yet-married girls were all home in the winter. After arranging for the girls to do the after-breakfast washing up, Florence made her escape saying she was off to run some errands.

Wilbur, Florence's favorite horse, was in the stall nuzzling around in the straw and as soon as he saw her coming, he held his head upright making gentle rumbling noises—his happy sounds. As usual, Florence laughed, thinking how much he reminded her of a giant purring cat. She greeted him with half an apple. He was always pleased to see her approaching with something in her hand. The horse had been a gift to her stepmother from a widower in the community who was sweet on her.

Wilbur greedily wrapped his mouth around the apple portion and Florence patted his neck. "We're going out today." When he was finished chewing, he nuzzled her, looking around for more treats.

"You can have more when we get home." She slipped the rope around his neck and led him outside in readiness to hitch him to the buggy.

ONCE THEY WERE clear of the driveway, Wilbur was just as pleased to get out onto the open road as she was. He held his head high as his legs moved into a steady trot, his black mane blowing in the wind. As she did every time she passed Carter's house, she did her best not to look. His car was outside, but she hadn't seen him since their kiss. That was entirely her fault because he'd asked her to come and see him the next day. She'd told him she would, but later she became too scared.

After a few minutes, she was well past his house, and she again focused her thoughts on her mother. Finding out about Eleanor was a good distraction to stop her thinking about Carter and what might come next.

Florence could understand why her brothers never talked about their mother, but was it normal for the whole community to remain silent? Perhaps it was out of respect to Wilma. Either way, she hoped by the end of the day she'd find out a few things from Mark.

WHEN SHE WALKED into Mark's store, she saw him behind his counter serving a customer. Isaac was working in the back room. Isaac spotted her and waved, and then left what he was doing to walk out to meet her.

"Good morning, Florence, it's nice to see you here. Can I help you with anything?"

"Hi Isaac. I'm here as a customer. I mean, …" She giggled. "I mean, I'm *not* here as a customer. I'm here to talk to Mark."

He rested his hands on his hips, smiling. "He should be finished in a minute." He gestured toward the back room. "Can I make you a cup of something? Tea, *kaffe?* We have a teakettle out back."

"I'm fine, but thanks. I won't be here for long."

He nodded. "I'm gonna get back to work or Mark will have something to say to me later."

"Of course."

He smiled before he headed back to where he'd been working. Isaac met her approval. He was genuine and kind. She hoped that someday he and her sister Joy would marry. They'd been practically inseparable the last few months except for when they'd had a small misunderstanding. Before Isaac came along, it was hard to imagine Joy with anyone. Isaac wasn't too bothered by Joy's impossibly high standards or her constant Scripture quoting.

With Mark still in deep conversation with his customer, she wandered around the store looking at the wide variety of saddles and bridles, and other bits and pieces they sold. He'd made a success out of the business and she was pleased for him. Running a business wasn't easy, something she knew all too well. They were doing well enough to employ an extra person, leaving Christina at home to run her own business of sewing prayer *kapps*.

When she heard Mark saying goodbye to the customer, she wasted no time in walking over.

Mark's eyebrows drew together in a worried-looking stare. "Hello, *Schweschder,* what are you doing here?"

She waited a second until the customer had walked out the store. "I've come to see you."

"Nothing wrong?"

"*Nee*, why?"

"Oh good. I thought there might've been. You've never stopped into my shop before." Now his normal happy expression was back. "I'm always glad to see you. I'll get Isaac to swap places and we can go out back."

"Okay, perfect. I do want to talk about something and it'll only take a couple of minutes."

He chuckled. "That's okay. We're in no rush today. It hasn't been that busy."

When Isaac had taken over in the shop, they

walked into the back room and sat at a small round table.

"So, what's it all about? You look bothered by something."

She cleared her throat. How was she going to approach this? It would've been easier if the subject of their mother had come up in conversation, but that was never going to happen. "Can I have a glass of water please?"

"Sure. Would you like me to make you a cup of *kaffe?*"

"*Nee denke.* Isaac already offered. Water will be fine." While he got the glass of water, she closed her eyes, summoned her courage, and tried to still her fast-beating heart. Was there something bad about her mother that she wouldn't want to know?

He sat back down placing the water in front of her. "You've got me curious."

She took a big gulp of water and set the glass back on the table. "The thing is, I wanted to talk to you about our *mudder.*"

His eyebrows rose, telling her that was the last thing he thought she might have come there to talk about. "Go on."

"Nobody ever mentions her. I don't have many memories of her. No clear memories and I wondered if you do." To encourage him to open up, she continued with the little things she remembered. "All I have in my mind is hanging onto the hem of her dress, and I remember her lifting me onto her hip. That's all. Most of all, I remember feeling happy. I think she was a cheerful person, but I don't even remember her face or her voice. What do you remember of her? I was two when she died. You were a few years older."

He scratched the back of his neck. "I don't have many memories at all—nothing much."

Her heart sank. "You must remember something." She sat still and waited for him to say something. Any little thing he remembered could help her fill in the blanks.

"I can remember us traveling in the buggy as a family. You were in the middle and Earl and I were either side looking after you. I can also remember us sitting at a small table in the kitchen while the adults sat at the big table. That's about all."

It was a let-down. He barely recalled anything at all. "Do you know if our parents were happy? Happy in their marriage and happy with each other?"

"I guess so. Why do you ask?"

She didn't want to shatter her brother's memories. Naturally, he would assume they'd been in love.

Neither could she tell him about the letter from Gerald Braithwaite—an apparent love-interest prior to their parents' marriage. Shrugging her shoulders, she said, "I was just wondering."

He drew his eyebrows together. "Why are you thinking about all this now?"

She thought quickly. "It's because of the girls getting married, I think. It's made me wonder what *Mamm's* life was like. Oh, come to think of it, there is something important I have to tell you."

"What's that?"

"I found letters that she wrote to each one of us before she died."

"What about?"

"In case she didn't live until we were adults—almost like she knew she'd die young. She said in my letter that *Dat* was to give them to us. He mustn't have gotten around to it."

"Did you bring mine with you?"

She slumped in her chair, feeling selfish and self-absorbed. *"Nee,* I forgot, sorry."

"I'd really like to read it."

"I'll get it for you and bring it to you."

"Okay. *Denke.* Do it when you get around to it, though. There's no rush."

"Okay, I definitely will. And I'll mail Earl's to him."

"Where did you find these letters?"

"In the attic among her things."

He rubbed his beard. "I didn't even know she had anything up there. I thought all her things would've been gotten rid of."

"*Nee. Dat* didn't toss them away, and Wilma never throws anything out. I helped Earl put *Dat's* things in the attic and that's when I saw *Mamm's* boxes. I had a little look through her things back then, but stopped." She knew she had to get to the point of why she was there. "It's frustrating that no one ever talks about our *mudder*. Do you know why that might be?"

He shrugged his shoulders. "Beats me."

"Who is the best person to ask about our *mudder?* Do you think Ada knew her well? She recently mentioned her to me, but we got interrupted right away so I don't know what she'd been going to say."

"I'm not sure. I'm not sure who knew her. I guess you could start with Ada—she'll be able to direct you."

"*Denke.* Good idea. I'll do that." She took another mouthful of water.

"Did you come here especially to talk about our *Mamm?*"

"*Jah,* I did. And to tell you about the letter."

Slowly, he nodded.

"I mean, don't you ever wonder about her?"

"From time to time, *jah,* I think about her and wonder what she would've been like."

"Why weren't we ever told anything about her?"

"Life goes on and *Dat* married Wilma. Wilma took over as our *mudder.* I'm sure she loved us as much as she was able, since we weren't hers."

"She did, and still does." She leaned in closer to Mark. "I miss her. I want to know her, but I never will. I feel slightly like I've been cheated." Tears formed in her eyes and she blinked hard. She'd barely talked to Mark alone since he'd married Christina shortly after their father had died.

"Do you think about her often?"

"Sometimes. Mostly, I just miss *Dat* because I knew him better, of course, and we used to go into the orchard every day and he'd teach me all kinds of things."

"You two were close." Mark laughed and seemed more comfortable now that the conversation was away from their late mother. "He wasn't blind. He knew you'd be the one to take over. Earl and I never liked the orchard, or farming of any kind."

"I don't know how that's even possible."

Mark shook his head. "You're so much like him."

"Am I?"

"Jah. You've got the same color eyes as he had. Even the way you twitch your nose when you don't want to say what's on your mind is the same as he used to do."

Florence laughed. "I never even knew that."

"It's true." He leaned forward. "What do you think of Isaac and Joy?"

"I think they make the perfect couple."

"We rarely see him at home. He's mostly over at your place for dinner every night."

Florence nodded. "He's already one of the family. I'd be happy to see them married. They suit each other just fine."

"I can't believe Mercy and Honor are married."

"Me neither. They're so young." Florence let out a sigh.

"There's nothing wrong with getting married young. See it as a blessing that they found the right person when they were in the prime of their youth. They can grow together in love and in *Gott's* ways."

Florence nodded. "That's right—it's a good way to look at it. I guess you're right."

"Of course I am," he said with an impish grin.

Florence giggled. She was no closer to finding out about their mother and what she was like, or why Gerald Braithwaite wrote that letter to her, but she felt better after talking to her big brother. "I should go and let you get back to work."

"Okay. It was nice to see you."

"It's nice to talk to you, just the two of us without being surrounded by people all the time." She stood up and so did Mark. He came around the table and gave her a quick brotherly hug.

"*Denke* for stopping by, Florence."

She gave him a little nudge with her shoulder. "*Denke,* Mark."

CHAPTER 2

When Joy heard the sound of a car on the driveway, she ran to the door and looked out. She was hoping it was Cherish, their youngest sister, somehow set free from the grip of Aunt Dagmar and her farm in the middle of nowhere.

It wasn't.

It was a delivery van! And the driver, sporting a baseball cap and baggy overalls, was opening the back doors of the van. Curious, she walked over to him. He looked up at her without a hint of a smile on his weather-worn face.

"Is this the Baker residence?"

"Yes, it is."

"I've got a flower delivery."

Immediately, her heart raced with gladness. She

was the only one in her family who had a boyfriend. Isaac, the kind and caring man that he was, had sent her flowers. It made her fall in love with him all the more. Even more delighted was she when the man pulled out a huge white box full to the brim with red long-stemmed roses. There must've been four dozen of them.

"I can't believe this. They're so beautiful. I can't believe he'd do a thing like this. He doesn't make much money and they must've cost him a fortune."

She giggled as the man put the box into her outstretched arms.

"Enjoy your flowers, Florence Baker."

"Florence?"

Neither his expression changed, nor the tone of his voice. "The delivery is for Florence Baker."

Her heart sank into the bottom of her boots. "Did you really say *Florence?*"

"Yes. You said this is the Baker residence?"

"It is," she snapped, due to the man being slightly intimidating.

"Does Florence Baker live here?"

"Yes, she's my sister."

"I'll leave 'em with *you* then." He turned to leave.

"Do I need to sign something?"

"No."

AMISH JOY

"Thank you," she called after him as he kept walking. He wasn't stopping for anybody; probably rushing off to the next delivery so he could finish for the day.

He looked over, gave her a brief nod, slammed the van doors shut, and got into the front seat.

Joy stood there with an armful of beautiful flowers as she watched the van head back down the driveway. Now she was bitterly disappointed.

Why couldn't the flowers have been from Isaac?

In the brief moment that she'd thought they were for her and from him, she'd felt special, loved. She'd always wanted the kind of man who would've done something surprising and delightful, like sending her flowers for no reason at all. Isaac had given her flowers before and they were beautiful, but that was a long time ago. As she stood there stunned and staring down the road, her two younger sisters joined her.

"Oooh, look at them," Favor said, reaching her hand out to feel them.

Joy moved the flowers away.

"Are those from Isaac?" Hope asked.

She turned to face her sisters directly, doing her best to hide her disappointment. "They're for Florence."

"Florence? Who would've given them to her?" Favor tugged the edge of the box.

"I don't know." Joy walked toward the house with her sisters on either side. When she was inside, she said, "I'll put them on the table so Florence will see them when she opens the door."

"There's an envelope there," Hope said.

"Let's see who it's from," Favor said with a giggle.

"Don't you dare touch that!" Joy was horrified at her younger sisters. "That note's for Florence. That would be as bad as opening someone's mail." Turning her back on them, she placed the small envelope next to the flowers before she turned to face them. "Don't touch the flowers or the envelope." Then she headed to the kitchen to help *Mamm* with the baking.

CHAPTER 3

FLORENCE FELT a little better for her visit to her brother. From his face, she had known he was still upset and affected by their mother's untimely death all those years ago. They both barely remembered her but that didn't mean they didn't miss her every single day. The most painful thing for Florence was that she didn't remember her face. How she ached for a photograph—a snapshot frozen in time. All she could do was guess what her mother looked like by looking at her two older brothers and from her own reflection. Somehow, she knew her mother had loved her like only a mother could; that was a comfort.

The boys had never been close with Wilma like she was. Wilma had tried hard, but the boys had never connected with her despite staying closely connected to their father.

It was for that reason Florence couldn't understand why neither of her brothers showed an interest in the orchard, but still, that had worked out better for her. Being older than she, one of her brothers could've easily taken over the orchard and where would that have left her? She preferred to be the one in charge and not the one who took orders.

Now the orchard was hers to run entirely alone. Her father had taught her everything he knew. If she was undecided about something, she'd almost hear his voice in her head, leading her and guiding her until she was satisfied she'd made the right choice.

It was a challenge running the orchard, the household and the store on her own, but it had to be done. Wilma wasn't capable of much. She was a different person now, ever since *Dat* had died. She used to be outgoing and cheerful, and now she seemed half the person she had once been.

As a treat, Florence stopped at a café and ordered take-out cappuccinos for *Mamm* and her sisters. After she ordered them, she waited for them to be made. Looking around the café, she saw that everyone was part of a couple. All of them, except for one woman with two toddlers she could barely control. Florence smiled at the children's antics, at the same time feeling sorry for the frustrated mother. She was reminded of the story Wilma told her of her sister who left the community after she found out she was pregnant. She'd later turned up on Wilma's doorstep, and Wilma had followed Amish custom and turned her away. Something, Wilma had said, that she regretted to this day. What had become of Wilma's sister and the baby? Florence knew that Wilma secretly hoped her sister would return one day.

"Miss. Miss?"

Florence turned around and looked at the barista, jolted from her thoughts.

"Coffees are ready."

"Ah, thank you."

She picked up the large tray with the coffees all fitted neatly in their slots to avoid spillage. Before she headed out the door, she got a few strange looks but, being Amish, she often got those. A nice man jumped up from his seat and opened the glass door for her, giving her a big smile. She thanked him and headed to her waiting horse and buggy.

On the way back home, Florence tried not to look at Carter's house when she passed.

Just a quick glance.

His car was still there, parked outside. Most likely, he was at home waiting for her visit, but she wouldn't go—couldn't go.

Even if she did, what could she do or what could she say?

The very act of appearing at his house would mean that she acknowledged that the kiss had meant something. And then what would happen? Things couldn't stay the same. There was nowhere for a relationship with him to go. No good direction, anyway. Only one where she'd be tempted to turn her back on the community and *Gott's* ways; she'd never allow that to happen.

From the things Carter had said, she knew he was an atheist, not a believer at all.

He had said his motto was *never say never,* but she couldn't let her future hinge on idle words from the mouth of an *Englischer*.

Deep inside, she felt the battle raging. Good against evil, the spirit against the flesh.

She desperately ached to see him again, but knew it would be the wrong decision to make. The best thing she could do was keep away.

It gave her a sense of comfort knowing he wouldn't come to her property and knock on her door. So long as she restrained herself, he would eventually forget about her.

It wasn't the same for her. She would never forget him and the special kiss that they'd shared. Perhaps she should've regretted it, but she didn't. It could possibly turn out to be the only real kiss she'd ever get.

Did Aunt Dagmar, *Dat's* never-married older *schweschder*, ever have one kiss? Florence smiled as she decided Dagmar had never gotten one. She seemed like the last woman who'd be tempted by a man. She was the perfect person for Cherish to stay with to learn some life lessons.

Cherish was Florence's youngest half-sister who had tried to run away, and then she'd been caught flirting with her older sister's husband-to-be. On Aunt Dagmar's isolated farm, there were no such temptations, only activities such as basket weaving and quilting to occupy her time once her assigned farming chores were finished.

When Florence pulled up the buggy at her house, Favor came running out toward her, followed closely by Hope. Her first thought was that there was some emergency or something had happened to *Mamm*. She jumped out of the buggy. "What is it?"

When she saw the girls grinning she relaxed, knowing everything was okay.

"You've got flowers," Favor blurted out.

"Big red roses," Hope added.

"Store-bought ones with long stems. They came in a big white box."

"With a big red bow."

Florence found their words hard to take in. "Wait! You said I've got flowers?"

"*Jah*, the note said *Florence*."

"They were delivered ten minutes ago. You just missed the delivery van."

She put her hand over her heart. Carter had sent her expensive red roses. This was worse than him knocking on her door. Trying to throw them off the track, she said, "I didn't think Ezekiel would do that."

"They're not from—"

Hope dug Favor in the ribs, and then said, "There's a note. We'll help you with the horse and buggy, won't we, Favor?"

"*Jah*, we will."

"*Denke*, that's very nice of you. I got us all cappuccinos."

Favor jumped up and down and clapped her hands. "Oh, goodie."

"*Denke*, Florence. How did you know I just now felt like one?"

Florence giggled. "It was a good guess."

As they worked to unhitch the buggy and then rub down the horse, Hope said, "I wonder if the person who bought you the flowers is the same person who left you the twigs Christmas before last."

Florence held in her laughter. "They weren't twigs. That was a rare grafted apple tree." He hadn't given her anything this just-passed Christmas, but he had expected her to visit.

"Looked like twigs to me," Hope said. "Where were you just now?"

"Yeah, we would've come with you if we knew you were going into town."

"I told you I was running errands. I also visited Mark at his store."

"Well you should've taken Joy if you were going there. She would've wanted to see Isaac."

"Isn't he coming to dinner tonight?" Florence asked.

"Most likely," Favor said. "But she still probably would've wanted to go with you and we would've gone too."

"Sorry, but it's too late now and you girls

wouldn't have finished your chores anyway. Grab your coffees and *Mamm's* too, and take them into the *haus* before they get cold. I'll finish up here."

CHAPTER 4

When Florence finally went into the house, the first thing she saw when she opened the door was the huge box of flowers sitting on the table at the opposite end of the room.

She walked forward. Nobody had ever given her flowers and these weren't ordinary. They were extraordinary—magnificent. Red roses were her favorite. How could he have known? She walked over to them and before she even got close, she breathed in their sweet aroma.

It was a heavenly scent, one like no other and almost good enough to eat. When she leaned forward to have a closer look, she noticed that many of the outer petals were so deep red in color that they were almost black. "These are the most beautiful flowers I've ever seen in my life." She turned around to face all of her sisters. "Can you smell them?"

"*Jah,* I smelled them," said Joy, handing her the take-out coffee. "They're beautiful."

Florence took the coffee cup and had a sip while Favor and Hope leaned forward to breathe in the scent of the flowers.

"They're pretty good," Favor agreed.

"Do you want me to put them in water for you, Florence?" Joy asked.

"I can do that." Favor took hold of the box and it was then that Florence spied the small envelope.

She snatched it off and looked at it. The heart-shaped sticker that was used to seal the envelope, had been torn; someone had opened it. Favor and Hope were hurrying into the kitchen and Florence guessed them to be the ones who'd done it. Florence placed her coffee down on the table and opened the envelope, hoping that Carter hadn't written down his name.

Beautiful flowers for the most beautiful woman in the world.

Your secret admirer.

. . .

HE WAS the only one who had ever called her beautiful.

She looked up at the girls who were now walking out of the kitchen and couldn't help putting her hand over her mouth and giggling. It was one of the happiest moments of her life.

Joy stepped forward. "Who's it from?"

"I can't say."

"Can't say because you don't know? Or you can't say because you don't want us to know?"

"You've opened it, haven't you?"

Favor and Hope looked at one another. "Are we in trouble?" Hope asked, looking ashamed.

Florence was in too good of a mood to punish them. "Not today. The note says from a secret admirer, and I know that you know that." She quickly put the note back in the small envelope.

When she walked into the kitchen, she saw Wilma up to her elbows in flour rolling out pastry for pies.

"I overheard it all," Wilma said smiling. "Secret admirer?"

"That's right. That's what the note said." Florence giggled. "Aren't they beautiful?"

"I've never seen roses like that in all my born days." Wilma gave her a lovely smile. "We don't have a vase to fit them. We've only got two small flower vases."

"I'll find something to fit." Joy rustled through the cupboard and pulled something out. It was a tall glass canister. "What about this?"

"That'll be perfect," said Florence. Then she proceeded to spend the next five minutes snipping a little off each of the stems while holding them under running water, and another five or so minutes arranging her flowers in the impromptu vase. She explained to her half-sisters that snipping the stems in this manner allowed the flowers to 'drink' the water in the vase, and they would last days longer. "I'm going to put them in the living room on the table where I found them."

"Who are they from?" *Mamm* asked.

"I don't know."

"Do you think they're from Ezekiel?"

Florence pulled a face at the mention of his name. *"Nee,* not after the letter he sent me saying things were too difficult because we lived too far apart." His rejection had been bitter for her to come to terms with, just when she'd been opening her heart to the possibility of liking someone other than Carter.

IN THE EARLY AFTERNOON, after the chores were done, Florence wondered what to do about the flowers. They must've cost him a fortune. The arrival of the flowers told her that Carter knew she wasn't going to visit him today, the same as every day since that kiss. He didn't want to be forgotten. She struggled with whether she should see him if only to thank him for the roses, but the problem was, where would that lead?

THE LATE AFTERNOON rain was a welcome sight for Florence. It wasn't a light sun-shower either. It was heavy enough to keep her inside. Without taking her walk, she wouldn't have her daily temptation of spying on Carter from a distance.

She sat home with the girls and *Mamm* as they huddled around the fire and hand-sewed baby clothing. It was something that *Mamm* had recently introduced.

"With Mercy and Honor now married, it won't be

long before the *bopplis* start arriving," she'd told them.

It was pleasant with only three of Florence's half-sisters at home now. Joy was the sensible one, older than her years. Hope and Favor were mischievous but only because they liked to have fun. There was no nastiness in any of them. Cherish was the brattish one whom Florence could barely tolerate; it was nice to have a rest from her spoiled and self-centered attitude.

The meat was cooking in the oven and soon they'd have to peel the vegetables.

CHAPTER 5

As usual when Isaac was coming to dinner, Joy did most of the cooking. She wanted him to know what a good cook she was, so he knew that when they got married he would not go short of a good meal. He liked his food and because he was a little heavier than most men, he had thought that she wouldn't be attracted to him. She had managed to let him know that, in her eyes, he was perfect, which truly was the case. She'd never met anybody that she'd gotten along with better than Isaac. He was the man she wanted to marry—when she was ready.

When Joy let Isaac in the front door, the first thing he noticed were the flowers.

"Roses?"

Still at the doorway, Joy turned to glance at the

flowers and then she looked back at him. "That's right." She leaned close and whispered, "It seems Florence has a secret admirer."

His eyebrows rose. "Florence?"

She nodded.

"Really?"

"It's true."

"Do you know who it is?"

"I don't, but he's someone with good taste judging by the flowers he sent." She watched him carefully while he stared at the flowers, hoping he'd realize that she'd liked to be surprised once in a while. It didn't have to be with anything expensive. Joy would've been happy with flowers picked from someone's garden. At least it would show he'd been thinking about her—caring about making her happy.

Then he smiled at her and asked, "What's for dinner?"

She wasn't satisfied that he'd appreciated the roses and gotten the hinted message she wanted him to receive. Linking her arm through his, she pulled him toward the flowers. "Smell them," she ordered, in a nice way.

He leaned forward and sniffed. "Very nice. But, not as nice as that dinner I can smell cooking. Is that a roast?"

Joy sighed. "It is."

"What's wrong with you? You don't look too happy."

"I am, Isaac, I am. Dinner won't be long."

"I know you're bothered by something. Is it because I haven't bought you flowers lately?"

She shook her head. "Don't be silly." It was true, but she didn't want to admit something that sounded so silly. "But they are beautiful, aren't they?"

"I bet you'd be pleased if they'd been from me. Is that why you look a little bothered? Are you jealous of Florence's flowers? Would you like to have a secret admirer too?"

She slapped his arm playfully as though that was the furthest thing from her mind. "No. Not now that I know you. And, I'm not jealous. It's not good to be jealous or envious. I could tell you where it says—"

He put his hand to his head. "Please don't give me all the Scriptures about jealousy. I know they're there. I don't need chapter and verse."

She poked him in the ribs with her finger causing him to laugh. "I won't. I'd never do that."

"You would too." He grabbed her hands. They had a quiet moment together while everybody else was in the kitchen. "Now, you can stop poking me. I'll have to hold your hands always."

"Okay. You can do that."

"Now, if I could only cover your mouth at the same time to stop you speaking, you'd be the perfect woman."

"Isaac! That's a dreadful thing to say."

"It was a joke." He chuckled. "Anyway, what did you do today?"

"Not much of anything except chores and cooking. How was work?"

"A bit slow. Florence was in the store this morning."

"Is that where she went?"

"It seems so."

"Why was she there?"

"She was talking with Mark in the back room about something."

"About what?" She led him over to the couch where they sat.

He shook his head. "I did hear them talking about their *mudder,* but I don't know if they meant Wilma, or their own *mudder.*"

"Is that so? What were they saying?"

He shrugged his shoulders. "I didn't hear it. I

wasn't going to listen in because that would be wrong."

"You're right."

He smirked.

"Come into the kitchen and talk to me while I make the gravy."

"We've only just sat."

"The gravy won't make itself. Everyone else makes the gravy lumpy. Do you like it like that?"

"I don't. Okay. I'll come, but we won't be alone anymore."

His words brought a smile to her lips and she forgave him for saying that thing about covering up her mouth. Even though she knew he was joking, it hadn't been a nice joke.

Once Isaac walked into the kitchen, he was swamped by Joy's two sisters, each of whom was talking to him at once. He ended up sitting down at the table while they hovered around him like buzzing bees.

Joy didn't mind. She was pleased he got along so well with her sisters. Even Florence seemed to approve of Isaac.

. . .

Over dinner that night, Isaac Joy a compliment. "You're the best cook." Isaac smiled at her.

Joy giggled. "What would your *mudder* say about that? I'm sure she wants you to think she's the best cook."

"Just as well she's not here, then, isn't it?"

The girls all laughed.

Favor said, "If you like Joy's cooking so much, marry her and she can cook for you every day."

Hope had a mouthful of water and she laughed so hard that it spurted out of her mouth.

"Hope! What do you think you're doing?" *Mamm* said in disgust.

"I'm sorry." Hope wiped her mouth. "She made me laugh. I couldn't help it."

"One more outburst like that and you'll have to leave the table."

"Sorry everyone," Hope said, as she mopped up the wet patch on the tablecloth with her napkin.

"It's okay," Isaac said sympathetically.

Joy noticed again how kind he was and knew he'd make a good father.

"Isaac, do you think the two of you'll get married?" Favor asked.

Joy kicked her under the table.

"Ouch."

"Stop it, Favor," Florence said. "It's not proper conversation for the dinner table."

Favor rolled her eyes. "You're not my *mudder,*" she muttered under her breath loud enough for everybody to hear.

"That's it!" *Mamm* said. "Up to your room." Favor's jaw dropped open, which wasn't a pretty sight considering she'd just shoveled in a forkful of food.

"Are you serious, *Mamm?* I'm only asking a simple question. I just want to know if they're getting married, and when."

"Up to your room now!" Florence told her, annoyed Favor hadn't listened to *Mamm.* "You heard *Mamm.* And if you don't go now, you'll be in your room all day tomorrow, with no visitors and you'll be eating your meals in your room."

"I'm going." She pushed out her chair and stomped out of the room.

Joy and Isaac exchanged a smile and kept eating.

Hope said, "When will Cherish be back? Is it fair to punish her for that long? I think she's learned her lesson by now. I miss her. It's not the same now that there's only three of us at home. And soon it might be… Well, it's just not the same."

It didn't escape Florence's notice when she said it

was three of them at home. Hope and the other half-sisters never considered Florence as one of them. Sometimes she just wanted to be the sister rather than a stand-in mother figure. She wanted to be included in their giggles, their stories and their jokes.

With Mercy and Honor now married, she was closest with Joy, the oldest sister left at home. She was in no rush for the youngest to come home; she was too busy to watch Cherish every single moment. That was exactly what would end up happening.

At Dagmar's farm, in the middle of nowhere, it was less likely that Cherish could get into any trouble. At least she had her dog for companionship, along with all the farm animals and of course Dagmar's budgerigar, Timmy.

Hope said, "Since no one answered me about poor Cherish. Can someone answer this? Are we all going to the charity auction?"

"Of course. When is it again?" Florence asked.

"It's the day after tomorrow."

"That came around again quickly," *Mamm* said.

"I can't go. I'll be working that day," Isaac said.

"That's too bad," replied Joy. "I'll buy some candy for you."

"Would you?"

Florence was slightly envious at the connection Joy and Isaac shared. They'd shared an instant connection from the first day they'd met. People who found love within the Amish community didn't realize how blessed they were. It wasn't easy having feelings for an outsider.

"YOU GIRLS CAN GO in a buggy on your own on Saturday," said *Mamm* a little later. "Levi has asked me to go with him."

"Really?" Hope shrieked.

"*Jah.* He's coming here and Bliss can go with you girls."

"Is there something you want to tell us, *Mamm*?" Hope asked.

"Careful that you don't end up in your bedroom like Favor." *Mamm* wagged her finger at her third youngest.

This was the first Florence had heard *Mamm* was going to the charity auction with Levi Brunner. He'd been visiting more and more over the last weeks. Was something going on?

It was no secret that Levi liked *Mamm*.

Was *she* growing fond of him, too?

As Florence ate the rest of her dinner, she

wondered if Wilma would ever marry again, and if she did, would it be to Levi?

She couldn't imagine Wilma being with anyone else but her father. It was uncomfortable to even think about.

Selfishly, Florence didn't want it to happen. Only because it wouldn't be a marriage out of true love, it would be a marriage of friendship and companionship. But, she had to ask herself, did that make it less important?

As Florence was contemplating love and marriage, Joy served up the dessert. When the bowls were all in the center of the table, Florence couldn't believe it. *Mamm's* apple pie was nowhere in sight.

Green jelly and whipped cream—that was all.

Joy served it out for everyone and Florence decided to give it a miss. She'd sneak herself some apple pie while doing the after dinner clean up.

The bright green wobbly jelly dessert looked far from appetizing, but the way Isaac was enjoying it she guessed Isaac had asked Joy to make it.

The girls didn't seem to mind the dessert, and *Mamm* never complained. Florence sat there while the girls ate their green jelly and talked about what they'd made for the auction.

CHAPTER 6

As they always did after they finished dinner with the family, Isaac and Joy headed out to the porch to speak alone. There they could hold hands and be close without the sisters giggling or Florence making 'behave yourselves' faces at them. Florence always watched over her and her sisters like a mother hen. It was stifling at times.

Once Isaac pulled the porch chairs closer together, they sat down. Then he reached out his hand and she clasped onto it. "That was a *wunderbaar* dinner." He gazed into her eyes.

"*Denke,* I'm glad you liked it."

"Who wouldn't?"

She giggled.

"I appreciate you making the green dessert. I know you only make it for me."

"I don't think anyone else likes it too much—they're not used to having sweeter desserts like that."

"It was amazing, just like you."

She giggled again at how corny he was, but corny or not, she could listen to him utter nice things to her all day long.

"How do you even make it?" he asked.

He certainly was preoccupied with food. "It's crushed and strained apples. I add sugar to sweeten the juice, then thicken it, and then it sets."

He chuckled. "I guessed that much, about the sugar, and how did you get the color?"

"Food coloring."

"Ah, that's the secret?"

"That's the secret to the color, but it doesn't affect the taste at all."

"I love it. Will you always make it for me?"

"Of course I will."

"I wonder why the others don't like it as much as me. None of them went for seconds."

"I've got no idea. It could be the color that puts them off, or they might not have been hungry after that big dinner."

He squeezed her hand. "When you cook for me, it lets me know you care."

She was surprised by his comment. "I care. You know I do."

"I know you do from your words, but it's nice to know as well from your actions."

"I learn more about you every day, Isaac." His words gave her goosebumps. It didn't matter what they talked about. Mostly, it was about nothing. "Everything new I find out about you makes me like you more."

"That's a relief."

"Will you be coming to the charity auction?" In the dim lighting, she stared into his beautiful face hoping they could have a whole day together. Charity auctions were always such a fun day out.

"I can't, unfortunately. I'm working that day—remember? I said so while we were eating."

"Really?"

"Yeah, and don't forget you said you'd get me some candy."

"Sorry! I can't believe I forgot we already talked about it."

"And, before you ask, I can't get out of it—your *bruder* is relying on me."

"I suppose. *Half-bruder*," she corrected him.

"I know that, but I didn't think I would have to say the half bit all the time."

"You don't. I'm just used to hearing it that way. You don't have to say that if you don't want."

"It saves time. How is Earl anyway?"

"I don't know. We barely hear from him."

"Ah, you're not close with him?"

"Not really, and it's not that I don't want to be. I think he's just too sad about *Dat* being gone. I don't think he's gotten over it yet."

"How about you?"

"None of us have ever got over it, but I can't run away like Earl did. I don't have a choice; I have to stay here at the *haus* with all the memories." She sighed.

He put his arm around her shoulder. "I'm sorry. I didn't mean to say anything that would upset you."

"It's fine. It's just the way things are."

"Life can be sad sometimes—even brutal. That's why we have to care for one another."

"What I've learned so far is that life is full of contrasts. It can be bad and it can be good. Happy, then sad, then it can get bad."

"That rhymes."

She smiled. "I didn't mean to make a rhyme, it just came out that way."

"That's right—what you say—it's all a cycle isn't it? Full of highs and lows. One minute life is boring and then when something bad happens you want to go back to the boring times."

"I think we should be happy with what we have." She saw him draw back. "Don't worry I'm not going to say a Scripture."

"You're not?"

She shook her head.

Isaac said, "There are a whole bunch of Scriptures about being happy—giving thanks for our daily bread and such."

"I know, but you've taught me that it's slightly irritating to constantly remind people of those things."

He chuckled. "I told you that?"

"You did."

"I don't remember saying anything to you."

She laughed. "You did. Just one or two things. I can take a hint pretty quickly."

"Well, I'm glad you weren't offended."

"You could never offend anybody. You're far too kind."

He gave a low chuckle.

"I know my sisters get irritated by me telling them about the Bible, so I've done my best to stop.

Even though it jumps into my head and I really want to tell people."

"Well, you're showing self-control, which is a good thing."

"*Jah*, self-control ... Proverbs ..."

He shook his head at her. Then he looked up into the sky. "It's a beautiful night, isn't it?"

"It's not freezing, or snowing, but it's close to freezing." Just then, gray clouds crossed in front of the moon. "It's so dark now." The only light was coming from the window behind them.

"It's gonna be a dark night." He yawned. "Sorry. I should go home soon."

"Okay. *Denke* for coming to dinner."

"I wouldn't miss it. You're all I think about every day when I'm at work. I can't wait to finish so I get to see you."

"Me too. That's how I feel. You're always on my mind. Do you think we'll always feel like that?"

"I don't know. We'll have to wait and see."

His answer worried her slightly. It wasn't what she'd wanted to hear. She wanted him to say they'd spend the rest of their lives together and be just as excited to see one another at the close of every day.

She didn't want to push him away by being too demanding and wanting him to commit to their love.

The best thing she could do, she figured, was to say nothing at all about his comment.

He bounded to his feet and she stood up too. "*Denke* for a lovely night, Joy."

"You're welcome."

He brought her hand up to his mouth and slowly pressed his lips on the back of it causing her to giggle.

"I'll see you tomorrow," he said softly.

"I'll walk you to your buggy."

"*Nee* don't. You stay here and wave to me from here until I'm out of sight."

"I will."

They exchanged smiles and then he left her and headed to his buggy.

She waved until the buggy lights were small in the distant blackness. Then with a bit of heaviness dampening her good mood, she walked back inside the house and closed the front door behind her.

"Has he gone already?"

"He has," she told *Mamm*.

She heard Florence in the kitchen and knew her younger sisters had gone upstairs to bed She sat down next to *Mamm* as she sewed.

Mamm gave her a sidelong glance. "Everything alright?"

The question took Joy by surprise. *"Jah,* why wouldn't it be?"

"You look a little pale and somewhat confused. Before that, you seemed to walk into the house with no spring in your steps."

"Oh."

"Are you coming down with something?"

"Nee. I feel perfectly fine."

Mamm wove her needle into the fabric and then folded up the white baby dress she was sewing. "My eyes are troubling me." She blinked a few times. "I might need glasses."

"You should go get checked out."

"All in good time. Right now, I'm off to bed."

Joy was a bit upset by her mother going to bed early. She had wanted to talk to her about a few things. There was no one else to give her advice with her two older sisters married and living a distance away.

Her mother walked over and kissed her on the top of her forehead. *"Gut nacht.* Can you tell Florence I said good night?"

"Jah, I'll do that. Night, *Mamm."*

When her mother walked up the stairs with her sewing tucked under her arm, Joy lay down on the couch and swung her feet up onto the armrest—

something she wouldn't be able to do if Florence or her mother were about.

Her two brothers-in-law had declared their love early in their relationships and had been desperate to get married, but Isaac hadn't done that. Did that mean he wasn't as much in love with her?

Then she remembered Florence's admirer. Joy couldn't help being slightly envious of Florence and those flowers. It was a feeling that she didn't like and was uncomfortable with, but still, she couldn't shake it.

Annoyed with herself, she sat upright with her feet now resting on the floorboards. In God's word, she'd find a Scripture to encourage her and bring her thinking back into line. His words would slice through the negative feelings swirling through her heart and her head.

CHAPTER 7

When Florence finished cleaning the kitchen, she walked into the living room expecting to see *Mamm* sewing, but even *Mamm* must've been so tired that she'd gone to bed. Florence had been keeping herself busy by doing extra cleaning in the kitchen. Wiping a dirty mark off one of the shelves had turned into pulling everything off the shelves and wiping everything down.

She glanced at the clock on the mantle and was surprised that it was after twelve; she'd guessed it was around nine thirty.

No one had come into the kitchen while she'd worked in there; not even to say goodnight. Still, at least the kitchen cupboards were clean and that saved her doing it another day.

She let out a yawn raising her arms over her head and then the sweet fragrance of her roses captured her attention. She walked closer to admire them for the fiftieth time since she'd gotten them.

Carter still cared!

However, she didn't need roses to remind her about him. He was never far from her mind or her heart.

She plucked a rose from the bunch, headed to the kitchen and filled up a glass. After she had shortened the stem by half, she popped the rose in the water and headed upstairs with it. Once in her room, she set the glass on the nightstand. A reminder of Carter might help her sleep soundly tonight.

She changed into her nightgown, took off her prayer *kapp* and unbraided her hair. Then she took hold of her boar bristle brush, sat on the end of the bed and brushed out her long hair all the while worrying what to do about Carter. When she had finished, she opened the window and looked out into the darkness in the direction of Carter's house.

Did he understand why she'd never come back to see him? She had to go to him, and she had to do it soon.

It filled her with happiness to know that a man like Carter liked her, wanted her.

No one before him had ever thought of her as special. In her youth, she'd been passed over. Even Ezekiel, the pig farmer, hadn't been interested. To have someone handsome and nice like Carter interested, made her feel worthwhile.

Soon, she had an important decision to make. Without him, her day-to-day life was monotonous. When he was close, that was when she truly came alive. It was the moments with him that felt like the truly important ones and she didn't know if it was wrong to feel like that.

Every moment since they'd shared that kiss, she was aching to see him again.

He felt that way too, she just knew it. He wasn't some lady's man using fancy words to try to seduce her or lead her astray like other *Englischers* had done to girls within the community.

If only she could dive into her future and get a glimpse of how everything would end.

It led her to wonder, did life itself have several possible endings depending on what decisions she made, or was it all predetermined? Was she in control of her life or was God?

She wiped her brow, somehow beaded with sweat, even in the freezing temperature.

If she ended up leaving the community for Carter,

would she be lost to God's grace? Would she find herself cast into the pit of fire after she died? That was what she had been raised to believe. She'd always thought it best to err on the side of caution, but that was before she'd met Carter.

In her heart, she knew not everybody fell in love so deeply.

This wasn't the kind of love that you could take or leave. It had taken over her mind, her heart and everything within her.

Maybe if she prayed real hard Carter would join them. That would be the perfect ending. She turned her head and stared at that single rose on the nightstand. It made her smile, but it needed something else. A solitary rose wasn't good enough. She was through with loneliness.

She crept down the stairs in the darkness and made her way to the roses. Reaching out her hand she felt carefully until her hand brushed a rose at the edge of the vase. When her fingers touched the petals, she ran her hand down to the stem, careful of thorns. Then she pulled out the rose and took it up to her bedroom.

Better to have two roses than one. The bunch wouldn't miss those two special roses that she kept in her room. She broke the long stem in half to fit in the glass, then tossed the lower half of the stem out her partially opened window.

When she popped the rose into the glass with the other one, she couldn't stop smiling. One was taller than the other.

One is Carter and one's me.

Feelings of love welled up within her, overflowed, and surrounded her. She closed her eyes and soaked it all in. She stood there for a good few moments, until the chilling breeze whistled through the window.

She hurried over to shut it and then looked through the window.

"Good night, my love," she whispered before turning to her bed.

After she slipped between the cold sheets, she turned off the gas light beside her. She'd forgotten to close the curtains, but that didn't matter. The light of the moon wouldn't wake her. It was a dark and cloudy night; the same as it had been for the last few nights. When her eyes closed, a hint of rose fragrance wafted under her nose and lulled her peacefully to sleep.

CHAPTER 8

Florence was doing the washing up after breakfast the next morning when she heard the faint sounds of a buggy—the rhythmic clip-clop of the hooves, and the crunchy sound of the pebbles on the driveway as the wheels rolled over them.

"Who's that?" Wilma asked, seated at the kitchen table.

The dark bay horse with its bright white star was a familiar sight at their house. "It's Ada."

"Ah, good. I'll put the teakettle on."

"I'll do it."

"Denke."

As Wilma went out to meet Ada, Florence shook her hands dry and then popped the mostly-full teakettle back onto the flame of the gas stovetop.

Minutes later, Ada was in the kitchen sitting with *Mamm*. Normally, Florence would've greeted Ada and then left the older women alone to talk, but before she could even say hello, Ada had asked her to join them.

Then Ada added, "Unless … you've got something better to do?"

"I've got lots of things to do, but I can take a few moments to have another cup of *kaffe*."

"Good."

Ada and her mother were so abnormally quiet while Florence made them a pot of tea that she knew something was going on. Once she had set the tea items down on the table, she sat down with a mug of coffee.

It didn't take long to find out what was on their minds.

Ada was the first to speak. "What's this I hear about you having a secret admirer?"

Florence steadied her mug so it wouldn't spill, as she giggled like a young girl. "It's not true."

"It is," Wilma said. "You saw the flowers, didn't you, Ada?"

"I surely did. They're beautiful."

She looked at the two women and knew that they had talked about it previously. It seems that *Mamm* told Ada everything no matter how small and insignificant.

"It's no big deal."

"Are they from Ezekiel Troyer?"

Florence shook her head. "Things are through with me and Ezekiel, didn't you know?"

"Jah, but I thought ... Who could they be from?"

"I wouldn't know for certain. It's a mystery." Florence hoped her face wasn't saying something different from her words.

Ada's eyes bored through her. "You don't know?"

"How could I know? There was no sender on the note that came with the flowers."

"Ah, that's a shame." Ada shook her head. "He was so well suited." She was still focused on Ezekiel.

"Humph," *Mamm* said with just the merest hint of a snarl. *"He* didn't appear to think so."

Ada opened her mouth in shock and asked Florence, "It was he who ended things?"

"Jah, didn't *Mamm* tell you?"

"Jah, but I didn't believe it until just now. Not that I didn't believe you, dear," she said to Wilma. "I just never thought that Ezekiel would've been the one to not persevere."

'*Persevere?*' Florence didn't like the thought of someone having to persevere with her. Or the thought that Ada was saying she hadn't tried to give a relationship with Ezekiel her best effort. "No words were said exactly, but I knew from his letter what he meant. Things were too difficult for the both of us to continue seeing one another with the distance between us. Then his *mudder* got ill, and on top of that, his *bruder* left the farm. It all became just too difficult."

Mamm said, "And she was all ready to go on that trip to see him and she had to cancel the bed-and-breakfast that she'd already paid a deposit on. I thought I told you all of that."

Florence felt horrible remembering everything about Ezekiel's rejection of her. In faith, and to do the right thing, she had decided to give him a chance. She'd opened her heart and booked the trip. And then the possibility of a life with him was over. A small part of her was pleased that she'd at least given him a chance.

"That's dreadful." Ada pressed her thin lips together. "That's not good enough. Did he at least pay you back for the deposit?"

"*Ach, nee.* I never let him know that I'd placed a deposit on the accommodation. I didn't want him to feel bad. When I got that letter, there was no reason to ever contact him again. I just want to forget all about it." She put her elbows on the table and clutched her coffee mug.

"I'm sorry Florence. If I had known that would be the outcome I never would've suggested him. I feel dreadful."

"Don't. I mean, it could've worked."

"She liked him," *Mamm* said as though she were helping matters.

"Anyway, all that's behind me now. And I'm looking forward to what the future might bring."

A mischievous twinkle came to Ada's eyes. "With your mystery man?"

"Maybe." It was natural for Ada to assume the man who'd sent those flowers would be an Amish man. Florence had little contact with *Englischers* with the exception of the apple customers.

"So, you want me to stop looking?" Ada inquired.

"*Ach!* You're not still looking for someone for me, are you?"

"I wasn't anymore, because I thought you and Ezekiel were well matched, but I could look if you want me to."

"*Nee*. That's fine. If it's going to happen …"

"Ada, find someone for her, would you?"

"*Mamm!*" Maybe another man would be a good

distraction to stop her thinking about Carter, or it could be another disaster. *"Nee,* Ada, truly I'm fine."

"I won't look for somebody but if someone comes to mind, I'll let you know."

Florence nodded. "That sounds like the best idea yet. Why don't you do that?" Florence took a large sip of her coffee, trying to put Ezekiel's rejection from her mind. She'd been rejected too many times in her youth. She wasn't sure why.

When Florence finished her hot drink, she left Ada and *Mamm* there to talk and left the house. With the girls in their bedrooms, Florence hurried to hitch the horse before her sisters asked where she was going.

CHAPTER 9

Florence hadn't seen much of her best friend, Liza, who was quite busy these days with her two young children. She hoped Liza had time for her today. She needed to talk. If not, she'd drive around the streets alone while she figured out what to do about Carter.

As she approached Liza's house, she saw her outside pinning out the washing. It didn't take Liza long to notice the buggy, and as soon as Florence pulled up in the yard, a fresh-faced Liza rushed toward her.

"Hello. This is great timing. I have the boys down for a nap—at the same time." She laughed cheerfully.

That was the best news Florence had heard in days. "Good. Can you spare a bit of time for me?"

"All the time in the world ... until one of them wakes up." Liza giggled. "Is something troubling you?"

Florence stepped down from the buggy and threw the reins over the hitching post. "Many things, but I don't know where to start." Part of her wanted to unburden herself about her attraction to Carter and part of her wondered if it wasn't best to keep it to herself.

Then there was the letter from her mother. She had to know what her mother meant about making mistakes. To do that, she had to find out more about her mother's life. "I want to know more about my *mudder*, and everybody seems quiet about her. For as far back as I can remember no one ever mentions her and I don't know how to find out more about her."

"I don't remember anything about her." Liza shrugged her shoulders.

"I know. I didn't think you would since we're the same age, but where should I go to find out who would know, and am I right in thinking there is some secrecy surrounding her?"

"Let's go inside." As they walked, Liza said, "I don't mean to be rude or insensitive, Florence, but she's gone, so why would people talk about her?"

"I wouldn't expect people to, but her close family

should still talk about her. I guess *Dat* didn't mention her because of Wilma. But he never talked to me about her, or to my brothers, and I just have a yearning in my heart to know her. I found a letter in the attic that she wrote to me a little while before she died."

"Really?"

They both sat down on the couch in the living room.

"*Jah*, and there was one for Earl and one for Mark."

"What did they say?"

"I haven't given them theirs yet, but mine didn't say much of anything really. Just something about following my heart and something like ... not making any mistakes."

"That sounds the same thing every mother says. I'll say that to my boys too. Us mothers just want to save our *kinner* from mistakes—protect them from everything."

"I guess."

"That's right."

She wasn't ready to tell her friend about Carter, she realized, or the letter from the *Englischer* to *Mamm*. She was certain her mother wouldn't want her memory tainted. Not that she had a reputation to uphold, what with no one talking about her, but if they found out about that, tongues might wag.

Florence sighed. "There are boxes and boxes of my mother's belongings in the attic. I had started to go through them when I found the letter."

"If you go through her things, that should give you an idea of the kind of person she was."

"That's what I thought. I should go back to that again, shouldn't I?"

"Why not? There's no point leaving things in the attic to gather dust. Why don't you see what things of hers you can use? It sounds like you need to have some of your mother's things around."

That was why she and Liza were friends. They thought along similar lines. "Exactly. That's why I started to go through her things. Her sewing machine is the only thing I've ever used. I wanted a cushion, or a rug—something I could keep in my bedroom, so I could feel her close."

"Is there anything else upsetting you?"

Liza wasn't silly, she knew there was something weighing heavily on her. Florence stared at her best friend hoping she wouldn't be too judgemental if she told her about Carter. "Well, there is one—" She was interrupted by the baby crying out.

"That didn't last long. I'll leave him be for a bit longer. What were you saying?"

"It doesn't matter."

"I made some white chocolate cookies yesterday."

"And, are there any left?"

Liza giggled. "I managed to rescue some of them. They're Simon's favorites. We can have cookies and tea."

"Sounds good to me."

They moved from the living room into the kitchen and Florence decided it was best to keep quiet about Carter. She'd figure out what to do. A large decision had to be made and it would be best that she make it alone.

"He'll call out like that for a few minutes and then he'll go back to sleep."

"Really?"

Liza nodded. "Hopefully."

Florence was silent. She didn't want to start telling her friend about Carter and then have to leave off in the middle of it. She took the baby crying out as a sign to keep quiet about it like she'd originally thought.

CHAPTER 10

THE NEXT DAY, thanks to the conversation with Liza, Florence was ready to head up into the attic to further explore her mother's belongings.

Her half-sisters had all gone to their friend Bliss's house to help sort out donations for the upcoming charity auction while Wilma was lying down in her bedroom with a headache. It was the perfect time for her to creep into the attic undiscovered.

WHEN FLORENCE WALKED IN, she was struck by the same musty smell from the other day. She lit the lantern that was just inside the door. The only daylight was from a small window in the roof. She walked over to the window remembering she had seen the roof of Carter's house last time she'd been there.

On her tiptoes, she looked out. Gray and white puffy rain clouds hung low in the sky over the two properties. As she stood staring, she wondered what Carter might be doing at this very moment. He still hadn't told her what he did for a living.

Even people from rich families had to work. Unless ... he was mega rich? But if he was, why would he be living on a farm away from everything? As much as she wanted to find out, it would mean going back there; if she did that, she didn't know if she could find the strength to keep resisting him.

She pressed her palm against the window pane, so it looked as though she was touching Carter's roof. It was the closest she could be and still remain safe until she figured out what to do.

After a deep breath, she headed back to discover what was packed into each of her mother's boxes. The first one she came to was a box of clothes that smelled quite musty after having lain folded in a box for over twenty years. Then she had an idea to go through everything little by little rather than try to discover everything at once. She took hold of the letters her mother had written to Mark and Earl and put them by the door so she wouldn't forget them.

After she peeped in the top boxes, she took a small box of clothes and the small carved wooden box where her mother's love letter had been. She snuffed out the light and made her way out of the attic.

In the safety of her bedroom, she went through everything in that box. Her mother's clothes were the same size as hers and she guessed that she and her mother would've been the same height, whereas Wilma was much shorter. It was comforting to know that she was a similar size to her mother and that they had shared something in common. It wasn't much, but it felt good to be the same as someone else. She didn't want to wear her mother's old clothes, but it was nice to see them and touch them. In a few days, she'd put them back in the attic.

Since there was no sign of Wilma getting out of bed yet, she took the small wooden box downstairs to sit in front of the fire, wondering what other secrets the box held.

She pulled out the letter on the top—the one from Gerald Braithwaite—and read through it carefully.

"How could you do this?" a voice sounded from the stillness.

Florence's head shot up.

It was Wilma, glaring at her.

CHAPTER 11

WILMA STEPPED FORWARD as Florence held the letter from her mother's love-interest in her hands. Then Wilma's gaze dropped to the wooden box. "Why are you going through that box?"

She wasn't sure why Wilma was so mad. Didn't she have a right to go through her mother's things?

"I just wanted to see what was there." Florence watched Wilma's cheeks and the tip of her nose turn beet red.

"What have you got in your hands?" she snapped, making Florence feel like a naughty two-year-old who'd been caught drawing on a wall.

"It's just a letter."

Wilma stepped forward and in an unusual and uncharacteristic rage, snatched it from Florence's hands and read it. Then she looked down her nose at Florence. "How could you? How could you make a mockery out of me?"

"Out of you? It's got nothing to do with you."

"It has everything to do with me. It wonders me that you were snooping in the attic without asking me, too." In an apparent outrage, Wilma lunged forward and tossed the letter into the roaring flames of the fireplace.

Florence let out a yelp and ran forward and made efforts to save it. She took hold of the poker and tried to move it away, but she couldn't. All she'd managed to rescue was a corner of the paper that had no writing on it at all. The piece had fluttered to the floor at her feet. She leaned down, picked it up and placed it in the palm of her hand.

As she stood there staring at the corner of the letter, *Mamm* scolded her once more. "What's gotten into you, Florence?"

Florence looked over at her stepmother and wasn't going to back down. Not when she wasn't in the wrong. "I could ask *you* the same thing."

"Don't go sticking your nose in where it doesn't belong."

"I could say the same to you." Florence was never

normally rude, but she was shocked to the core by what Wilma had done.

"Florence Baker, if you weren't as old as you are I'd send you to your room."

"And if you weren't older than me and my stepmother besides, I'd have a few things to say to you as well." Florence tossed the fragment of paper into the fire. It might as well be lost too. Without words, it was no good.

The women then stared at one another.

They'd never had cross words like that before—ever. After a while, Wilma turned and walked into the kitchen and Florence sat back down staring at the fire.

Now she knew why *Dat* had never mentioned her mother in front of Wilma. She obviously was extremely jealous of her mother—unreasonably so.

WHEN WILMA STOMPED up the stairs a few moments later, Florence was so disturbed and upset that she ran out of the house. This was the first argument she'd ever had with Wilma. The only place of solace and comfort was in the midst of her orchard where no one would see her.

Once she was well away from the house, she held

onto a tree and sobbed. Her very life's foundations were crumbling around her. She didn't fit in with her father's new family, as much as she'd tried she'd always felt an outsider. Now, she knew exactly why Mark and Earl had left.

Wilma had been a mother to her and mostly they'd had the same view of things. Sure, they didn't agree about everything but nothing had ever before caused Wilma to have an outburst like she'd just had.

Why couldn't Wilma see that it was reasonable she go through her mother's things and read her mother's old letters?

Why was it so bothersome to Wilma?

She knew she would feel better if she talked to Carter. Just being near him would make her feel whole again. He would agree with her, Florence was sure about that. Any reasonable person would be able to see her point of view.

Now that she'd given herself permission to see him, she couldn't wait. Instead of walking, she ran in the direction of his house. Once she got to the last tree of the orchard's border, his house came into view.

She looked and stopped still.

His car wasn't there and that meant he wasn't home.

She was devastated, and knew in her heart she shouldn't have waited so long to see him. What if he'd left and she'd never see him again? Tears spilled down her cheeks. He was the only happiness she had. She couldn't lose him. With the end of her apron, she wiped her eyes.

Life was hard sometimes, and lately Florence always felt like she was making the wrong decisions.

Pushing Carter out of her mind—for now—she headed back to the house.

With her mother having gone back to bed and her sisters out, it was a perfect opportunity to visit Ada and try to find out more about her mother. First, though, she grabbed the box and tiptoed up to her room to put it where Wilma wouldn't see it. She'd look through it later.

It was more than clear she was never going to find out anything from Wilma.

CHAPTER 12

Florence knocked on Ada's door and waited a moment. When no one came to the door, she called out, "It's me, Ada. It's Florence."

Ada opened the door and looked surprised to see her. "Sorry, I was just out back. Were you knocking for long?"

"Not long."

She glanced over at the buggy. "You're here without Wilma?"

"*Jah,* she has a bit of a headache."

"*Ach,* that's no good. She's getting a few of those lately. She'd get a few more if Cherish was still here." Ada chortled. "Is there anything I can do for her?"

"She'll be fine. She's in bed and the girls have

gone into town to get a few things, cotton and wool, I think. They're making things for the charity auction and also, *Mamm* thought we should get in early and start making baby clothes for Mercy and Honor's *kinner* when they arrive." Florence giggled. "They've been busy and staying up late at night. It has been fun."

"*Jah*, and that's a good idea."

"I just wanted to talk to you about something if I might?"

"Of course." She stepped back and opened the door wider. "Come through to the kitchen. I was just cooking, but that can wait."

"I won't hold you up long."

"It's fine. I've got all day. Samuel's at the Wilson's helping with their fence."

Florence followed her through to the kitchen.

"Can I get you some meadow tea?"

"*Nee, denke.* I've just had something at home."

Once they were both seated at the round wooden table, Ada asked, "What was it you wanted to ask me?"

"I wanted to ask you about my *mudder*?"

Ada almost choked. "Your *mudder*?"

"*Jah.* I wanted to know what she was like."

Ada stared at her for a moment, and then a smile

appeared around her lips as she leaned back. "She was a whole lot like you."

"You mean in looks?"

"*Jah.*"

It pleased Florence to know she looked like someone. She'd figured from her *Mamm's* clothes that they were the same size at least. "Were my parents in love?"

"As far as I know." Her face screwed up. "Why do you ask?"

"I just feel I've come to the age where I want to know more about her. No one has ever told me anything about her. Everyone's been quiet and it's like there's a veil of secrecy surrounding her. It's starting to annoy me."

"Have you asked Wilma?"

"*Nee,* not straight out."

"Why not?"

"I just feel she'd get upset." She didn't want to tell Ada about the tantrum her stepmother had just thrown, tossing the letter written to her mother into the fire. Then Florence realized that Wilma probably had thought it was a love letter from her father to her mother and maybe that was why she was so upset. "I just get the impression Wilma is uncomfortable that *Dat* had been married before—maybe.

That's why I'm asking you what you know about her and what she was like."

"She was a *gut mudder*. She loved her *kinner* and she was a pleasant woman."

"Is there anything else you can tell me about her?" Florence hoped to find out about this other man.

"Not really. She was just the same as any other woman in the community."

"She wasn't a good friend of yours?"

"Nee, she wasn't."

"Any particular reason?"

"Not really. I had my friends and she had her friends."

Florence took a deep breath. "And what about before my *mudder* married my *vadder?*"

"I'm not sure what you mean."

"Did she have any other suitors—any other boyfriends?"

"That's going back a bit far for me to remember." She tapped her forehead. "Let me see now."

"Think hard. It's important."

"Nee, I can't think of anyone else. Why does it matter so much?"

"It's just that I wanted to know about her."

"Are you thinking about Ezekiel again?"

"Ezekiel?" The question came as a shock. "I'm not thinking of him at all."

"I thought maybe you were thinking about how many boyfriends your *mudder* had before your *vadder* so you'll know how many boyfriends you should have before the right one comes along or something."

Florence shook her head.

"Don't mind me."

"It's just that I wanted to know about her because she was my *Mamm*."

"I still think Ezekiel would've made you a good husband."

"Yes, you could be right about that. He might have made me a good husband, but it just wasn't to be."

"You could've tried."

"*Nee*, Ada, he ended things with me. I was willing to try. Remember? I even—"

"*Jah*, I know, but it's just such a shame."

Florence couldn't agree verbally, so she just nodded to keep Ada happy. "So, *Mamm* didn't have any other boyfriends besides *Dat* that you remember?"

She shook her head. *"Nee."*

"Oh. Do you know anyone who'd remember more about her?"

"Not really. She was an outsider, so that's why—"

"What? 'An outsider?' You mean an *Englischer?*"

"*Jah,* that's right."

"Oh! I don't know what to say. I never knew anything about that. So that's why I don't have grandparents, cousins, aunts, or anything on my *mudder's* side?"

"That's right."

"I never even thought … I feel so silly. I mean, I bet I do have all those relatives, but I just don't know them yet."

"Yet? What's the point?"

"They're relatives."

"Relatives of a woman you don't even know."

"I do know her. She's my *mudder.*"

Ada stayed quiet and looked at her with sympathy.

"Did anyone say to keep this a secret from me and my brothers?"

"Not that I'm aware of. *Nee.*"

"That still explains the secrecy I suppose. She joined the community for love. How romantic." Florence couldn't help but smile. Maybe her mother had joined for some other reason, but she wanted to believe it was for love. *"Denke,* Ada."

"I didn't tell you anything."

Florence giggled. "You did so. You told me more than anyone else has. I wonder if the bishop could tell me more."

"I'd say he'd be the one."

"You're right."

"Are you sure you wouldn't like something to eat?"

"I don't want to hold you up."

"I made a batch of peanut cookies this morning."

Florence loved Ada's cookies. "I might try one, or maybe two."

Ada stood up and walked over to the countertop and lifted a tea-towel. "They're still a little bit warm."

"Yum."

Florence stayed there for a while longer, chatting with Ada to avoid going home and facing Wilma.

CHAPTER 13

OVER THE NEXT few days things didn't improve with Florence and Wilma. Her stepmother said nothing at all about the letter or her fit of temper. Then the day of the charity auction arrived.

Every time Florence had gone to see Carter, his car hadn't been there. That had made her feel on-edge and nervous.

Had she left things so late that the decision over Carter had been taken out of her hands completely? *Not to decide is to decide.* She'd once heard someone say that, and now she could clearly see the truth in it.

Florence wasn't comfortable about her mother going to the auction with Levi. He was clearly head over heels about her and Florence wondered if her stepmother might marry him, if he asked, just to keep him happy. That was the kind of thing she'd do. She always wanted to keep people happy and not upset anybody.

Florence intended to wait for a quiet moment and then she was going to ask Wilma what her thoughts were about Levi, but finding a quiet moment in their household wasn't always so easy.

If Florence made the first move to talk with her stepmother, maybe it would break the tension between them.

All the girls were now leaning on the porch railing waiting for Levi and Bliss to appear. They were ten minutes late and Florence glanced over at *Mamm*, knowing she wouldn't appreciate his tardiness. She could tell by Wilma's upturned nose and pinched-looking face that she wasn't happy.

Still, *Mamm* probably wouldn't say anything to Levi. She'd keep it to herself and it would be one silent strike against him. Florence felt slightly wicked acknowledging that she was pleased about that.

Mamm had never shown interest in another man since *Dat* had gone home to *Gott*. Levi was the one doing all the chasing. Florence often heard the girls giggling between themselves about their mother and Levi. They certainly didn't seem concerned and they'd never, to her knowledge, discussed that they might have a new stepfather.

Levi and Bliss eventually turned up fifteen minutes late.

Bliss jumped down from the buggy and ran over to greet the girls. Florence walked over to her waiting buggy and got in. As she collected the reins in her hands, she stared at Levi. *Mamm* sat in the seat beside him and Florence watched as Levi's mouth moved up and down making all kinds of apologies.

Mamm smiled and nodded and seemed to be telling him it was okay, but it wasn't. Not when the girls still had to set up their stall with the apple goods they were donating. The only reasonable excuse for *Mamm* would be if someone was dead, or a tree had fallen down on the road and blocked the way. No flimsy excuse would do.

Once the girls were in Florence's buggy, Favor yelled. "Let's go!"

"Okay, but not so much screeching. Good morning, Bliss."

"Gut mayrie, Florence," Bliss said. "How are you?"

"I'm fine *denke,* and I'm looking forward to a good day."

"It should be."

By this time, Levi and *Mamm* were already

halfway down the driveway.

"Quick, catch up with them," Hope said leaning forward.

"Yeah," Bliss agreed. "Don't let them get away."

Florence giggled. "I'll do my best."

To keep the girls happy, Florence caught up with them and followed along behind them.

"Pass them, pass them," Hope said.

"In a minute, I'll see if I can."

When she passed Carter's house she noticed his car was there, but all she could do was look out of the corner of her eye. She didn't want to let the girls see her interest in their neighbor.

Florence urged her horse faster and pulled out and passed Levi's buggy. The girls were screeching with laughter as they passed and waved to *Mamm* and Levi. Normally, Florence wouldn't have bothered, but it didn't hurt for the girls to have some fun. Her mood was much brighter now—she had seen Carter was home. She knew in her heart she'd see him soon.

She knew the apple goods they were selling at the store were already packed in the buggy in an organized manner. Even though they were arriving later than she'd hoped, they should have enough time to set up the stall before people would start arriving.

CHAPTER 14

Without Isaac at the auction, Joy was doing her best to enjoy it. She and Favor had taken the first shift on the stall selling their apple produce, and then Bliss and Hope were doing the second shift after they ate an early lunch.

Late in the morning, Hope ran toward Joy.

"Did you see Isaac?"

"He's working."

"*Nee!* I saw him. Mark donated a saddle to the auction and he's here. He's here!"

"Where?"

Hope looked around. "I don't know. I can't see him now but he's here somewhere."

Her day was saved from being horrible. Unless it

was all a joke. "I'll find him if he's here. Swap with me?"

"No way! It's half an hour before I have to start."

"Just do it for me and I'll do something nice for you sometime."

Hope rolled her eyes. "Okay. I guess I can."

"Denke."

She wasted no time in hunting him down. If he was donating something, he'd be in the auction tent. She saw him in the distance coming out of the tent. He looked up and saw her and they rushed toward one another.

"You came after all."

He laughed. "I know. I wanted to give you a surprise."

"I'm so pleased you're here. I didn't know if Hope was tricking me. I'm so happy now."

"Me too."

They stared at each other for a while and she desperately wanted to hold his hand but she knew he wouldn't do that. Not in front of this many people.

"How was the stall?"

"Good. We sold out of apple pies, and we've sold a lot of other things too. We'll have to bring more next time."

"The auction is going to start soon. Will you sit with me?"

"Of course I will."

"I saw your *mudder* with Levi."

"I know. They came here together."

"Really?"

"He came to collect *Mamm* and then Bliss rode with us girls. I told you what was happening."

He shook his head. "You might have told me when I wasn't listening." He scratched the side of his face. "It seems they're getting close. You might have a new *Dat* soon."

"Yeah, I've thought about that and a step-*schweschder.*"

"How would you feel about that?"

"It would be different. We all get along with Bliss. She's a bit noisy, though, kind of like Favor."

"That might not be a good combination, two of them like that in the same *haus.*"

"Cherish was a lot worse."

"Poor Cherish. I kind of feel sorry for her. Don't tell your *mudder* I said so."

"I do too, a bit, but I'm sure she's having fun at the farm. She's learning to make baskets and all sorts of things. Aunt Dagmar is a nice lady."

"She is your *vadder's schweschder*, right?"

"That's right." Then she said, "I do miss Cherish's dog, though."

"Do you?"

"*Jah*. It's nice to have a pet around the *haus*. Makes it feel more like a home."

"What about your cats?"

"They're barn cats. They don't like to be inside and they don't like to be touched. They're hunters. They like being outside."

"I know how they feel. I like being outdoors too."

She laughed and slapped him playfully on the shoulder. "It's not really the same thing."

He laughed along with her. Then he touched her arm and guided her to the auction tent.

"Who's working in the shop?"

"Christina volunteered to help so I could bring the saddle here and surprise you."

Joy was shocked. "That was nice of her."

"All my family is nice."

She smiled at him. She couldn't tell him that Christina wasn't always that friendly—she was surprised that he didn't see that for himself. It was probably hard for him to see it, though, since Christina acted so differently around him and Mark.

Now she thought she knew what the problem was. Christina was upset that she didn't have a baby and they had been married for a while. It couldn't have been easy for her, if she wanted one so badly and hadn't become pregnant yet. That was Joy's best guess as to why Christina was odd. When she and Mark first got married, she was odd because she thought *Mamm* didn't approve of her. *Mamm* wasn't too happy about the marriage but only because they had gotten together on *rumspringa* and she had her doubts that Christina was a match for her stepson.

CHAPTER 15

THE GIRLS, including Bliss, had told Florence they would look after the stall—two would be on duty in the morning and the other two in the afternoon. That left Florence free to wander about and to watch the auction.

Florence would've rather been kept busy because she had no one to wander around with. Liza wasn't going to be there, and Florence really wasn't that close with anyone else in the community. Once she and her childhood friends had grown up, they had all gotten married and had babies. Naturally, they'd grown closer bonds with the other married women in the community. It was only normal, as they had so much more in common with each other, but Florence couldn't help seeing it as another rejection in her life. Only her very best friend, Liza, had remained close.

Florence had helped the girls set up the stall and then they all told her to stay away and they'd handle it all. "You go and enjoy a day off," Hope had said. That showed her they were acknowledging how hard she always worked.

As Florence walked past one of the small refreshment tents, she noticed her stepmother and Levi had teamed up with Ada and Samuel to have a bite to eat. The last thing she wanted to do was join them, so she filled in her time looking at the stalls and talking to the stallholders.

She was grateful when midday arrived and the main auction started. She sat down on a chair, feeling painfully alone in the crowd, and watched as all the donated items were auctioned.

At two o'clock everyone started to go home, and Florence couldn't have been more ready to pack up the stall and go home, too. At a suitable time, she'd steal away and see Carter to thank him for the flowers.

Then she saw a familiar figure. She stared again, to make sure. There was no mistake.

It was Carter and he was walking toward her.

Her legs were suddenly heavy and refused to

move even though her head was willing them. Their eyes were locked onto one another's.

"Carter! What are you doing here?" He was as handsome as ever in faded jeans and a white long-sleeved shirt.

"I heard there was an auction. It's for charity, so I thought I'd come along and see if I could donate some money—make a donation or buy something. What are you doing here?"

She stared at him. "You knew I'd be here, didn't you?"

He smirked. "I was hoping. I can't knock on your door, or call you."

She stared at him awkwardly hoping no one would see them together, resisting the urge to look around to see if anyone had noticed them.

He pulled lightly at his collar. "Florence, you can't deny what happened between us."

Even there, in plain sight at the fairground, she wanted to hug him, touch him, be close with him. It was like the rest of the world stopped when they were together. Nothing else mattered. "I have no intention of denying it."

"I think you have every intention of doing so. You don't think we fit together but we do."

"It's complicated."

"You think your life is complicated but my life is not?"

"I don't know anything about you or your life because you still haven't told me anything about it. I barely know anything about you." She shook her head.

"Is that the problem?"

"Problem?" She put her hand to her head hoping she wouldn't faint again like the last time she'd seen him.

"Is that what's keeping us apart?"

"I think it's obvious, the biggest thing keeping us apart, don't you?"

"Whatever it is it's nothing that can't be overcome. You can leave the Amish to be with me." He flashed her a smile and she couldn't help but giggle.

"If only it were that easy." He was so carefree and relaxed and she wanted a piece of that.

"It's easy! You take off your bonnet and the rest of your costume, wear normal clothes and come live with me."

She shook her head. "I'd never live with—"

"Marry me, then? There, I've never asked anyone to marry me. What do you say?"

"I have a whole life, a whole other different life compared to you. You can be free and not give anything else a second thought, but I have a family to take care of. An orchard."

"And, so do I. Well, not the orchard part. People usually do have their lives full and mapped out for them, but if they're lucky enough to meet someone special they adapt and make changes to fit that person in. I'm willing to do whatever it takes to have you in my life, Florence."

She stared into his eyes. Did that mean he might be willing to join the community? Probably not, but it wasn't something that they could discuss standing here in the middle of the fairground while she was worried about who might see them talking. What a scandal could arise!

"Can we talk about this later?"

"We could. I've been waiting for you to come and see me since I can't make contact with you. Something tells me you'd be a little upset if I came to your house."

She nodded emphatically. "That wouldn't be a good idea."

"I figured as much."

"I'll come and see you soon."

"Do you promise?"

"I said I would, so that's as good as a promise."

"Okay, Florence Baker, I will hold you to your word even though you said you'd come visit me the last time I saw you and you didn't."

"Didn't I?"

"No. Otherwise, I wouldn't have allowed you to leave."

His words pleased her and she tried to hide her smile. She had to change the subject or she'd burst with happiness.

"Did you end up buying anything at the auction?"

"I bought a couple of small things."

"Thank you for your contribution."

"That's the least I could do to help the firefighters. They do a wonderful job."

"Yes, they do. Thank you for the beautiful flowers. They were spectacular."

He smiled and stared into her eyes. "What do they say, 'a rose for a rose?' Bye, Florence."

"Bye." She didn't want him to go and wanted to tell him so, but right there in the middle of the fairground surrounded by members of the community, she couldn't.

He turned and walked away from her. What

would happen if she threw caution to the wind and left everything to be with him? Biting down hard on her lip, she resisted the urge.

She still didn't know if that kiss had been a big mistake or the cornerstone of a new beginning.

If what they had was real, it would wait. Wouldn't it?

She couldn't leave it to chance. Her feet started moving and her mouth opened to call for him, but just then …

"Florence, who was that?"

She turned to see Wilma and stopped still. "Ah, that's our nextdoor neighbor." She hung on to the strings of her prayer *kapp* to stop her hands from fidgeting. Her whole body buzzed with nervous energy.

Mamm looked over at Carter as he walked toward the parking area. "Oh! I would've thanked him for what he did for us, if I'd known. Why didn't you introduce me?"

What was *Mamm* going to thank him for? All Florence was focused on was the kiss Carter and she had shared. "Thank him for …?"

"For what he did for Honor, bringing her home that time."

"Oh *jah*, that. I've already thanked him. I didn't see you coming or I'd have made the introductions."

"I'm inviting a few people back for dinner. Do we have enough food to go around?"

"*Jah*, of course."

Mamm smiled.

"I guess that means Levi and Bliss are coming?"

Mamm nodded. "And a few others besides our usual guests."

CHAPTER 16

When they came home from the auction, Florence tended to organizing food for the dinner. All she wanted to do was be with Carter, but she couldn't leave when they had guests for dinner. As well as Bliss and Levi, there were several other people *Mamm* had invited. Joy was helping her in the kitchen while *Mamm* talked with everyone in the living room.

While Joy mashed the potatoes, she said, "I didn't know he was going to be there today. He surprised me."

Florence froze. "Who?"

"Isaac of course. Who else would I be talking about? He said he wasn't going to be there deliberately to surprise me. Wasn't that nice of him?"

For a moment, Florence had thought she'd somehow meant Carter. "It was. It must've been a lovely surprise for you."

"He's so thoughtful like that. You like him, don't you, Florence?"

Hmm. She was talking about Isaac again. "Of course I do. I like him very much."

Since Christina was one of their guests, Joy whispered, "He's so friendly—nothing like Christina."

"I'm sure Christina does her best," Florence said, not liking to say anything bad about someone.

Joy wrinkled her nose. "I guess so. She's improving a little. What are we having besides potatoes?"

"I'm making a stew with what we've got."

"They call that pot luck stew."

Florence giggled. "We also have some leftover fried chicken I can heat up."

"*Wunderbaar!* And I have loads of green dessert jelly."

Florence grimaced at the strange dessert Joy had concocted. "I guess we could offer that as an option and also cut up some fruit, and we've also got cake."

"Good idea. Green jelly is Isaac's favorite." Joy giggled.

Nearly every second word that came out of Joy's

mouth was about Isaac, but Florence couldn't blame her. She was thinking about Carter just as much. The good thing for Joy was that she didn't have to worry about being in love with an outsider or the burden of making a difficult decision.

Favor walked into the kitchen. "Can I help in here? They're talking about boring stuff out there."

"Sure. Joy will give you something to do."

"I don't want to peel potatoes. I always end up cutting myself."

"Well you're not helping if you only want to do what you want to do," Joy told her.

"I offered to help. I thought you'd be pleased."

"Thank you. It was nice of you since it's not your night to cook."

Favor grunted. "I thought you could use more hands."

"That was very kind of you," Florence said, "and Joy has finished the potatoes and she's already mashing them."

Joy giggled at Favor.

Favor put her hands on her hips and glared at both of them. "How did I know what she was doing?"

"There's really nothing much, but you can help me set the table soon."

"Okay."

As her younger sisters talked amongst themselves, Florence couldn't help thinking about Wilma and Levi. Tonight, she'd keep a close eye on them to gauge how close they were.

If Mamm married Levi, she'd move to Levi's house with all the girls and she'd be left in peace to run the orchard.

That was a perfect scenario for her.

Peace and quiet.

She'd never lived by herself, but she knew she'd love it. Without the constant distractions of her family, it would be too easy to see more of Carter.

THAT NIGHT they had dinner at the larger dining table rather than the smaller one in the kitchen.

From where Florence sat, she had a good view of her mother and Levi who were sitting beside one another.

The dinner conversation centered around the day's events, which was only natural. The auction had raised over $15,000 toward the firefighters. That was a lot more than last year and everyone was excited about that.

Bliss said, *"Dat* was a volunteer firefighter years ago."

"Were you, Levi?" *Mamm* asked.

"I didn't know you were," said Samuel.

"I was, for a few years until I hurt my leg. I fell off a ladder in the barn and did something to my leg."

"What did you do to it?" Ada asked.

"I don't know. But it's given me a limp."

"You didn't go to the hospital?" Florence asked.

"Nee. I've never gone to them. I don't like the places. *Gott* looks after me, and it wasn't his will I be a firefighter any longer."

Florence studied each person in turn. *Mamm* looked thoughtful, probably wondering what would happen if she married Levi and got sick. Would he refuse to take her to a doctor. Then there was Joy with a smirk hinting around her lips, probably thinking of all the scriptures she could quote.

Favor was eating with her mouth open, most likely not even listening.

Hope's eyes were wide, wondering something similar to *Mamm.*

Isaac was looking at the ceiling, hoping there would be green jelly for dessert.

Christina looked bored as though she wanted to go home.

Mark looked disturbed, probably because he knew Christina was ready to leave.

Then Florence looked over at Ada and Samuel. Ada looked like she wanted to comment and was holding back, and Samuel was frowning with his head hung low.

After another silent moment, Florence couldn't take it anymore and said the first thing that came into her head, "You'll all be pleased to know there's Joy's green jelly for dessert."

"*Wunderbaar!*" Isaac said. "My favorite."

"I guessed it was," Florence said.

"We do have more besides the jelly, don't we, Florence?" *Mamm* asked, blinking rapidly and trying to hide her distaste.

"A lot more choices for the non-jelly-lovers."

"All the more for me," Isaac looked over at Joy and smiled.

Florence decided that, if *Mamm* married Levi, she'd have them all to her place for dinner every so often. It was nice to have everyone gathered together for fellowship and a meal.

It wasn't long before she thought about Carter again and wondered what he was doing right about now. He mentioned he couldn't cook even though he had a brand-spanking-new kitchen that had cost a fortune, when all he really needed was a microwave. He'd told her he heated his food rather than cooked it.

In her mind's eye was a scene of him in his kitchen getting his dinner and sitting alone to eat it. Then after dinner, he went back to his computer to play his chess game.

AFTER DINNER AT THE BAKERS' *haus*, Florence asked Hope and Favor to wash up. Bliss volunteered her help. Florence figured there be more giggling going on rather than work. No matter. At least she could join the adults in the living room and continue to keep that close watch on Wilma and Levi.

CHAPTER 17

By the time Florence left the kitchen, the only seat left in the living room was one next to Christina. Florence wasn't happy about that, but she decided to make the best of it.

"How are your prayer caps doing?"

Christina smiled. "Really good. I have a large order for them from one of the shops in town."

"That's really good. Are you continuing to get many other orders?"

"I do. All my friends have ordered them."

"I'll know where to go when mine wear out."

"Don't you make your own?"

"I do, but I've been sewing other things lately."

"Like what?"

She lowered her voice so the men couldn't

hear. "Wilma's got it in her mind that Mercy and Honor will soon be having babies. Well, I suppose they will, and she's got us all making baby clothes."

Florence noticed that Christina didn't look at all happy now.

"I see. I don't have any *kinner* so that's why I'm able to spare the time helping at the saddlery store and making the *kapps*."

"That's very convenient."

"No it's not," she snapped. "There is nothing convenient about it at all."

There was a hush over the crowd as everyone stopped their conversations to stare at Christina.

Florence felt a bit sorry for her sister-in-law.

"I'm sorry, that's not what I meant to imply," Florence told her.

"That's alright. I'm tired—I haven't had much sleep lately."

"*Nee?* Why is that?"

"I don't know. If I knew the problem I could solve it."

Florence laughed. "That's a very good point."

A smile tugged at the corner of Christina's lips. "You should help me to sew some *kapps* to help me fulfill that order."

"I'm sorry, but I don't have the time. Maybe one of the girls can do it. Joy is good at sewing."

"Don't worry about it. I would've paid you, of course. I would share some of the money with you."

"That's very generous, *denke,* but by the time I do everything around here and keep everything stocked for the store and do all the orchard chores it doesn't leave any time."

"I understand. It was just an idea."

"*Denke* for thinking of me anyway."

She gave a curt nod. "So, what's new with you, Florence?"

There was nothing new with her that she could talk about. And the last thing she would do was talk about Carter with Christina. "There's nothing new."

"What happened to Ezekiel?"

"That fizzled out months ago."

"He was here just recently wasn't he?"

"A while ago. He didn't even come to Honor's wedding, remember?"

She shook her head. "I'm sorry, I didn't notice."

"That's okay, I didn't think that you would."

Christina studied Florence for a moment and her eyes flickered with anger. "What's that supposed to mean?"

"Nothing. There were just so many people at the

wedding, I don't think I even saw all the people who attended."

Slowly Christina nodded as she accepted the answer. "That's true. You're right. There were a lot of people there. I didn't even know half the people who were at my wedding."

When Christina smiled, Florence was relieved.

CHAPTER 18

THE NEXT MORNING was Sunday and today there was no meeting. When Florence was washing up the breakfast dishes, she heard the girls squealing about something.

"Will you stop it?" *Mamm* called out. "I can't take the noise anymore. You all gave me a headache yesterday with your constant carryings on. Can I have one day of quiet?"

"There's a car coming," Favor called out.

Florence looked out the window and saw a black car heading up their driveway.

"It's Mercy!" Favor squealed.

"And she's by herself," Hope yelled out.

Florence froze to the spot. This was what she'd

feared, and it'd come true. Mercy had married too soon, without the two of them learning about each other first, and now they were already separated. Wilma would be distraught. She'd believe it was a bad reflection on her family.

That meant Mercy would either have to reconcile with her husband or stay single forever. It would be a dreadful life for her. She looked around for *Mamm*, but she was outside with the girls waiting to welcome Mercy.

Florence quickly dried her hands on a hand towel and stepped outside to join them. Mercy was getting out of the car just as the driver was taking two bags out of the trunk.

While all the girls ran over to Mercy, Florence sat on one of the porch chairs watching the whole scene play out as though she were an outsider. That was how she often felt.

Then she heard someone ask where Stephen was. Mercy said that Stephen was working so she had taken a couple of days to visit.

Florence wasn't convinced by that flimsy excuse. The distance was too great from Wisconsin to travel for a couple of days, and why hadn't she visited before now? She'd only been back for Honor's wedding.

The girls and *Mamm* walked into the house with Mercy and sailed right by her. Not one of them gave her a glance as she sat on the chair.

That made Florence feel worthless, made her wonder why she was even there working so hard at the orchard, working so hard in the house, providing them an income and a nice place to live—and got no gratitude or recognition in return. And now with *Mamm* barely talking to her since the letter incident, except to complain that Florence hadn't introduced Carter to her, it made her feel even further away from the family.

Just then someone rushed toward her; she looked around and saw it was Mercy.

"There you are." She bent down and hugged Florence and Florence patted her on her back.

"What brings you back?"

"Just a little holiday."

"The others might believe that, but I don't believe that for an instant."

Mercy look bothered by that. She glanced over her shoulder to see if anyone could hear and then she crouched down next to Florence. "I was gonna wait for the right time to tell everybody—perhaps over dinner tonight but I'll tell you if you won't tell anyone else."

"Go ahead."

She whispered, "I'm pregnant."

Florence nearly cried with happiness. "And that's what you've come to tell us?"

"*Jah*, I was hoping to come with Stephen, but he just can't get away from work. I thought it was best to come and tell everyone in person because when we left we planned to be coming back in a year and now we're not. Do you think *Mamm* will be very upset?"

"I think she will be extremely upset, but she'll come to understand that you have your own life to live now that you're grown up."

"I hope so. Are you pleased for me, Florence?"

Florence sprang to her feet and hugged her oldest half-sister. "This is the best news I've had since … since I can't remember when." She held Mercy at arm's-length and looked at her. "*Jah,* you do look kind of glowing. And what's married life like?"

"Perfect, just perfect, just like I hoped it would be."

"I'm so glad to hear that."

"Come inside with everyone but don't say anything yet. I'll tell them all over dinner."

"I'll come in, but I'll just sit out here for a minute if that's okay."

"Why? Aren't you feeling too well?"

"Just very tired and you know how noisy the girls are. I'll be in in a moment. I'm very happy for you, and for me." Florence giggled.

"*Denke,* Florence. If it's a girl I'll call her Florence." She laughed. "Just kidding. That's a bit of an old-fashioned name. I'll call her something modern and different."

Mercy ran into the house, giggling while Florence shook her head. *Typical Mercy.* She hadn't changed at all. Maybe motherhood would change her.

Florence looked out over the orchard. Since *Mamm* still wasn't talking to her, she almost felt like a stranger in her own home.

She wasn't as close to her half-sisters as she would've liked to have been because they saw her as more of an authority figure rather than a sibling or a friend. But this was her home, and it was more her home than it was Wilma's. *Dat* had raised his first family there before he'd married Wilma.

When laughter and screeching came from inside, Florence knew Mercy hadn't been able to keep the secret until dinner time like she'd said.

The laughter and loud talking went on for a few more minutes and then Wilma appeared on the porch. "Florence, come inside and hear the good news."

She turned to see Wilma's smiling face. "I heard. She told me on the quiet."

Mamm stepped closer. "You knew?"

"Only a minute before everybody else."

Wilma rushed at her, leaned over and hugged her. Still sitting in the porch chair, Florence was trapped and couldn't move. She patted *Mamm* on her back, figuring this was her way of apologizing.

When *Mamm* straightened, she said, "*Ach*, Florence, in faith we all made *boppli* clothes and now my prayers have been answered. I always wanted more myself, but this will make up for the *kinner* I didn't have."

"*Ach, Mamm,* six was a good number. And you had me and the boys to raise."

Florence wondered if her mother realized that Mercy and Stephen wouldn't be moving back for a while. The longer they stayed, Florence guessed, the easier it would be to settle in the community where Stephen was raised.

"I know, but still …"

"Congratulations, you're going to be a *grossmammi.*"

Wilma giggled. "I will, won't I?" Florence nodded and then Wilma gave her a big smile. "Come in soon?"

"*Jah.*"

Wilma turned and hurried back into the house.

CHAPTER 19

FLORENCE EVENTUALLY WENT BACK inside the house and Joy helped her prepare the dinner. Since it was Sunday, the day of rest, they were having last night's leftovers to keep the work to a minimum.

Once everyone was seated at the table, all was quiet until Mercy spoke. "Can Cherish come back while I'm here, *Mamm?* I'd love to see her. I haven't seen her since Honor's wedding."

"It'll cost too much to have her driven here and then back again."

Favor said, "Allow her to stay here, then."

"I'm not willing to do that until I'm sure she's learned her lesson."

"I'm sure she would've learned her lesson by now."

"I'm not so sure."

"You've gotta give her another chance, *Mamm*," Favor said.

Florence interjected, "We gave her another chance and she didn't pass the test."

"I just feel sorry for her, stuck all the way over at Aunt Dagmar's. It seems awful to just leave her there like she's unwanted, uncared-for and ... and unloved."

"We do love her," Florence said. "We just love her more from a distance."

Mamm giggled at Florence.

"I'm only joking, Mercy," Florence told her. "We do miss her, but we also want the best for her."

Mercy said, "So, is it your choice to keep her away?"

Mamm shook her head. "It's both of ours. Florence and I both agree that it's not the best thing for her right now to come home. We'll know when the time is right. You need to trust your *mudder*."

"I would just like to see her, that's all. I thought I would see all my sisters while I'm here. I hoped I would anyway."

"You can always write to her," Hope said. "Like Favor's pen pals."

Favor frowned at Hope. "You have pen pals, too."

"Not as many as you."

Mercy said, "I do write to her and she writes to me. That's why I know she hates it there."

Florence wondered if Mercy was also there to plead Cherish's case for her.

Mercy sighed. "I just think ... it's just not fair that's all."

"Wait until your *boppli's* born. Then you'll have to see that sometimes you have to make some tough decisions in order to keep them safe."

Florence was pleased that *Mamm* was finally speaking her mind. Normally, Wilma left things like that to her. "How are you liking where you're living, Mercy?"

"I like it a lot. I like Stephen's family." Mercy giggled. "Jonathon is upset because he is the oldest brother and he's not having the first grandchild."

"Wait a minute," Hope said. "I thought Stephen was the oldest."

"*Nee*, silly. Stephen is the middle one."

"It's so confusing." Hope stole a piece of chicken off Mercy's plate when she wasn't looking.

Favor said, "If you think that's confusing, how do you think people can remember the six of us? The Wilkes only have three sons."

Hope shrugged her shoulders and popped the chicken into her mouth.

"Honor said she'd have a *boppli* before me and I said she wouldn't. I was right."

"It's not a competition," *Mamm* said.

"*Nee,* but Jonathon started it. It's a race now and we're beating them."

Florence hoped and prayed that Jonathon would prove her wrong; that he'd turn out to be a good husband, and one day, a good father. Every time she heard his name, she cringed.

CHAPTER 20

The girls were walking upstairs to bed, and *Mamm* and Florence stayed in the living room. Florence wanted to ask why she had been so upset over the letter. Many widowers remarried and that should take nothing away from their first wife or their second. She knew her father had loved Wilma very much, but didn't know if he'd loved his first wife, her mother.

Didn't she have a right to find that out?

She didn't want their argument to be swept under the rug and never talked about again. *"Mamm,* about the letter the other day."

"I don't ... I'm sorry for what I said to you."

"What you said?"

"You know, the argument we had. We shouldn't

let things like that come between us. I overreacted when I saw you with that letter."

"I said some things and I'm sorry too."

"Let's put it behind us and forget it. We've got a lot of bright things coming in our future."

Florence nodded. They did have a lot of good things in their future. "I'm going to be an aunty. It seems hard to believe."

"Well, you better believe it."

"I do want to talk more about the letter before we never talk about it again."

Mamm stared at her. "Not now. Please, not now. We can talk about it another time."

"Okay, *denke*. I really do want to talk about it, though."

"We will."

Florence was glad that they were friends again. She pushed her annoyance away and stood up and gave her stepmother a hug. "Did she say anything else?" Florence asked.

"Who?"

"Mercy, when she told you she was pregnant?"

Wilma narrowed her eyes. "No, like what? She's not having twins, is she?"

Florence laughed. "Not that she told me, no, I don't think so. I don't think there's anything else. I was just wondering what else she might have said." Florence wanted to know if Mercy had told her mother that she wasn't moving back. "Bedtime for me now."

"Night, Florence."

"Gut nacht, Mamm." Florence walked upstairs and saw Mercy and Joy giggling in the hallway. "Nice to have you home even if it's just for a few days, Mercy."

"It's nice to be back."

CHAPTER 21

Joy wasn't ready for sleep. "I've put your bags in my room, so we can talk all night."

Mercy pushed the door open. "It's my room, don't forget that."

"Not anymore. I've taken it over. It might've been yours once."

"We'll call it *our* room." Mercy flopped onto the bed and lay down.

"*Nee.* It's *my* room and you can stay here as my guest."

Mercy rolled her eyes and sat up. "You haven't changed. You're still as precise as ever."

"*Denke.*"

"It wasn't a compliment."

"If it wasn't, it should've been. We can talk until morning."

"Not all night. I need to sleep for the *boppli*." She patted her tummy. "I want to catch up on everything, but I'm a bit tired from all the traveling." She looked down at her stomach. "I suppose he can sleep any time."

"He?"

"I'm sure he's a boy."

"That's exciting. Let me feel your stomach." She put a hand out to feel Mercy's stomach and Mercy batted her hand away. "Stop it."

"I'm just trying to see how fat you are."

"I'm not fat at all, yet. It's too early for that."

Joy changed into her nightdress. "You're fatter in the face."

"I don't know why. I've lost weight with all the morning sickness."

"Morning sickness?" Joy screeched. "You're not gonna be sick all over me in the morning, are you?"

"Not if you wake up early and bring me tea and toast."

Joy rolled her eyes. "Okay, I will. What time do I have to do that?"

"As soon as I tell you to do it."

Joy shook her head and then took off her prayer *kapp*.

"I'm going to enjoy being home." Mercy removed hers, too, and lay down on the bed once more.

"Do you make Stephen look after you with toast and tea and all that?"

"I don't *make* Stephen do anything. He wants to do things for me."

"I hope my husband will be like that." Joy took hold of the bags that she had brought upstairs earlier and pulled out a night dress for Mercy. "Are you going to be staying long enough to unpack, or are you just here for a day or two?"

"Leave all that, I'll do it tomorrow. I'm here for a couple of days."

"Okay."

When both girls were in their nightclothes, Joy brushed Mercy's hair. It was just like the old days before Mercy got married and moved away.

"Is it crowded at the Wilkes's home?" Joy asked.

"We moved out of Stephen's parents' home."

"You didn't tell me that."

"I don't tell you everything."

"I know that. There's lots of things you haven't told me."

Mercy giggled. "I'll catch you up with everything before I leave."

"Please do. Now it's your turn to do my hair." She passed the brush over and the girls swapped places. "Where are you living now?" Joy asked.

"We're renting a little house not far away from Stephen's folks. It got pretty crowded once Honor and Jonathon came to live there."

"And how do you like the community there?"

"It's okay, but it's not home."

"It's been over a year since you married and you told us you'd only be there about a year."

"Plans change, people change, ideas change."

"What does that mean?"

"It means we might not be back for a while."

"Obviously, because it's been about two years already."

"I know. I will have to tell *Mamm* tomorrow. I think she thinks that we'll be moving here before the *boppli's* born. I didn't want to have to tell her outright. I wanted her to guess before I had to tell her."

"What are your plans for tomorrow?"

"I'm going to ask Florence if I can take one of the buggies. I'm going to visit all my friends. You can come with me."

"That's okay. I've got something else planned." Joy couldn't think of anything worse than visiting Mercy's friends. If Mercy was taking one buggy, she'd ask if she could take the other. Her plans involved finding out if Isaac was planning a future with her. Who better to find out from than Christina, his sister?

CHAPTER 22

THE NEXT DAY, Joy stood on Christina's doorstep and knocked on her door. Christina opened the door and stared at her. "Are you here by yourself?"

"I am. Mercy has come home with some exciting news. She's pregnant."

When Christina's eyes popped open in surprise, Joy realized that Mercy should've been the one telling Christina and Mark. After all, Mark was their half-brother. Now she'd ruined it. "Whoops. I should've let her tell you and Mark."

"Did you come over especially to tell me, or did you want to talk to Mark? Mark's at the store."

"I came to see you, but not about that."

"Should be interesting. Come on inside." She opened the door wide. "You won't mind if I keep working, will you? I've got an order for fifteen of these *kapps* and I need them finished for tomorrow afternoon. I've got six to go."

"Do you need some help?"

"I've seen your sewing, so, no."

Joy was startled by her comment, but still, she wanted to like Christina because she loved Isaac. "I like your honesty."

Christina led the way back to a sewing machine in the middle of the living room and Joy sat on a chair behind her. This was going to be awkward. Joy had been hoping to get information out of Christina in a conversational way but that was obviously never going to happen. Not while she was sitting behind her. It was weird. "Mercy's baby will be your niece or nephew." Christina grunted and Joy thought she hadn't heard, so she said, "Are you excited about being an aunt, Christina?"

Christina spun around and glared at her. "Do I look like I'm excited?"

She didn't. There was no hint of a smile around her pinched face. *"Nee,* you don't."

"How long has she been married?"

"Well over a year. Two maybe."

"And how long have I been married?"

"You?"

"Jah, how long have Mark and I been married?"

"Um, must be more than three years by now."

"You should know, you were there."

There it was again, Christina's prickly personality. "I know it was over three years because you got married not long after *Dat* died."

"You're right."

"I'm sorry I don't remember exactly when, Christina. I've got a dreadful memory sometimes. Don't be angry."

"I'm not angry at you." She shook her head. "I'm just annoyed. *She* gets pregnant almost immediately and I'm still waiting. I'm not happy."

Joy found it hard to understand her attitude but tried to see things from her point of view. It would've been frustrating to be trying and failing to get pregnant, but couldn't she be joyful for someone else and share in their pleasure?

When Joy could find no words to comment, Christina said, "I know you think I'm awful, but I don't care. I'm upset. I wanted to get married so I would have a family and where is that family now? All I've got is a husband and a *bruder* living with me. Where are my *bopplis?* My faith is wavering, Joy, it's wavering. If *Gott* is kind and loving, can't He see my pain?"

"He won't disappoint you. He will come through. He came through for Sara and Abraham."

"From the Bible?"

"Jah." Joy smiled trying her best to be encouraging.

"Oh good, I'll be a *mudder* when I'm over eighty."

"Um, that was just an example. There are also lots of places in the Bible where it tells you just to have faith. Have faith like a grain of mustard seed and that faith will grow big like an oak tree." Joy had been caught unawares. Normally, she had the Scriptures at the tip of her tongue but today, Christina was making her extremely nervous.

"Did you come to preach at me? The Amish don't allow women to preach, so … You think you're doing something right, but you're not."

Joy rubbed her forehead. "I wasn't preaching."

"It certainly sounded like it to me and you're also showing off. You're trying to show me that you know the Bible better."

"Well, I'm sorry. That wasn't what I was meaning."

"Joy, tell me something."

"Sure."

"Exactly why are you here?"

"Because we are family and …"

"That's right, you thought I'd be overjoyed about your *schweschder* having a *boppli* when I'm sitting here barren sewing these stupid prayer *kapps*." She stood up and ripped the material out of the sewing machine and threw it onto the floor. Then she took the scissors and started cutting into the finished *kapps* that were lined up on the sewing table.

Joy bounded to her feet. "Stop! Stop, Christina!" She grabbed Christina's arm and Christina started to cry. While she was sobbing, Joy managed to work the scissors safely out of her hands and placed them back down on the table.

Christina sat there and wept into her hands. Joy leaned over and put her arms around her and then Christina sobbed some more. There were no words Joy could speak in case she set Christina off again, so she remained silent and allowed Christina to cry.

Then she remembered her father told her that sometimes the best way to communicate with someone was to say nothing at all. This, she thought, was one of those times. Unless her father had said that merely to stop her from talking.

After a few moments, Christina's sobs got fewer. She sniffed and pulled away from Joy. "I'm sorry. I can only imagine what you think of me now." Christina dried her face with the end of her apron.

"I don't think anything of you, apart from you being my *schweschder*-in-law who keeps my *bruder* happy." That wasn't what she thought of Christina, but if she said those things in faith, it might come true.

"I hope I do."

"Of course you do. He's wonderfully in love with you."

That brought a small smile to Christina's lips. "I try to be a *gut fraa,* and a *gut schweschder* to Isaac."

"And you are. Isaac is so grateful that you allow him to live here and have given him a job at the store."

"He's a good worker, otherwise, we wouldn't keep him on." She managed more of a smile. "Even though he's a relative."

Joy took a handkerchief out of her sleeve and handed it to her. "It's clean."

"Denke." Christina unfolded the handkerchief and wiped her eyes. "Now I've ruined this *kapp.*" She picked up the tatters of what was once a head covering. "And all the others."

"How about I help you? I'm not too good on the machine, but I'm a pretty good hand sewer."

"Are you?"

Joy nodded. *"Jah."*

"How good?"

"Pretty good."

"Then I'd appreciate your help if you could stay here for the next couple of hours and help me out."

"Sure, I can do that."

"How about you start by making us a couple of sandwiches?"

"Sure." Joy stood up. "I've never had a real job before."

Christina stared at her. "You won't be paid for this."

Joy giggled. "I don't want to be paid."

"Good."

"Two sandwiches coming up."

"There's leftover roast beef."

Joy headed to the kitchen, found the meat in the gas-powered fridge, and made the sandwiches. Now that she was staying there longer, she'd have a good opportunity to find out more about Isaac.

AFTER THEY'D FINISHED their sandwiches, Christina gave Joy some sewing to do. She watched Joy for a few minutes. "You're not too bad, Joy."

"*Denke* ...I think. Does that mean we're friends?"

"Not yet."

CHAPTER 23

Joy couldn't find out any information from Christina. She arrived home with sewing that she'd agreed to do for Christina. There was too much work for one person, so *Mamm* and Florence offered to help after dinner.

That night, Isaac came for dinner again and after dinner, Joy seized the opportunity to work out where she stood with him. More than anything, she wanted their relationship to last and needed to hear he wanted the same.

She'd led him out to the porch and she sat on a chair while he leaned against the railing in front of her.

"Wouldn't it be the best thing in the world to be having a child?"

"You've got that right. I suppose it's okay for some but the person would have to be ready for it though."

"Who wouldn't be ready for it once they were married?"

"A couple who weren't married."

"Oh, that's silly," Joy said. "That goes without saying."

"Does it?"

"I think it would just be the most wonderful thing in the world. I hope it happens to me one day." She looked up at him from under her lashes.

"Me too."

"Really?"

"*Jah,* I hope it happens for you too, if that's what you want."

This wasn't going how she'd pictured it. "It's *Gott's* plan for everyone."

"Well, not for everyone because there are people who don't get married."

"Most people in the community get married."

"That's right and I'm not talking about those who do."

She did her best to hide her frustration. Didn't he see what she needed from him? "But don't you want to get married someday?"

"I do. When everything is right and everything is ready."

"What things?"

He left the railing he'd been leaning against and sat down beside her. "Just everything. Everything has to be right and in the right time, in the right place."

She had no idea what he was talking about; didn't he think that she was the right person? Was that the problem?

She didn't ask anything further through fear he'd tell her what she didn't want to hear. That night they hadn't held hands and now Joy was so upset she didn't want to. "I guess we should be going inside now. It's getting cold."

"Sure, I'm right behind you." He jumped up, and held out his hands to pull her from the chair. When she stood, he pulled her toward him for a hug, but she stepped aside and walked into the house.

He left soon after and Joy knew he was unaware she was upset.

◦

WHEN ALL THE girls had gone to bed that night, *Mamm* and Florence were still working on the hand-sewing for Christina's prayer *kapps* while sitting opposite one another. "I'm sorry for the other day, Florence."

"That's okay. We both said we were sorry last night, remember?"

"I do, but there's one thing I can't figure out."

"What's that?"

"Why were you reading my *schweschder's* letter?"

In shock, Florence jabbed the needle into her thumb. She quickly checked, glad there wasn't any blood. *"Nee,* it was my *mudder's* letter."

"Nee, it wasn't. It was from the horrible man who got my *schweschder* pregnant."

Florence put her fingertips to her forehead as she thought back to the contents of the letter. There had been no Christian name mentioned. The only name was from the sender. "Are you sure? I thought, when I read it, someone wanted *Mamm* to run away with him."

"My *schweschder* was going to marry a man from our community and was all set to do so, but then she got pregnant and left us. I don't know where she went and I don't know what happened to that dreadful man. She couldn't have gone back to him because I'm sure she was destitute that time she knocked on my door." *Mamm* shook her head and looked down. The memories were obviously painful.

"Wait, that letter wasn't to my *mudder?*"

"*Nee.* Your *mudder* and *vadder* married when they were quite young. They never had eyes for anybody else."

"They were in love." The words tumbled out of Florence's mouth without her thinking first, like they so often did.

"Did you think otherwise?"

She looked up at Wilma. "When I saw that letter, I had my doubts. I mean it seemed like that man who wrote that letter was very much in love. He wrote it like he was loved back, but the woman had decisions to make."

After a quiet moment, Wilma said, "That's why you were so upset with me? You thought I was throwing away your *mudder's* letter."

"That's right I did. Why was your *schweschder's* letter with my *mudder's* things?"

"It's not only your *mudder* and *vadder's* things stored in the attic. I have a few boxes of her things up there, too. When she left, she left everything. And when I moved here, I brought them with me. *Dat* said to put them up in the attic. I suppose I should've told you that, but I didn't know you were up there."

"This is certainly a shock." Florence closed her eyes and rubbed them. It was a lot to take in. "Hold on a minute. She got pregnant by a man with the last name of Braithwaite?"

"That's right. I can't say for certain, but that's my best guess. What of it?"

Her stepmother didn't know their neighbor's last name. "Nothing. It's just an unusual name, that's all."

"I've never heard it before either."

"Do you know anything about this man?" Florence asked.

"Just that he was a dreadful, dreadful man."

"Why was he so bad?"

"Because of what happened. He talked her into doing dreadful things. Things like that should only be done when people are married."

"Well, that's the ideal, but sometimes it doesn't happen like that."

"Does that mean you think I'm awful for turning her away the day she came to the *haus*?"

"I can just see two sides of a thing. I know you were doing what you thought to be right at the time. That's all a person can do."

Wilma nodded and looked down at the floorboards.

"Tell me this, when she knocked on the door was she pregnant?"

"She would've had the *boppli* by then, and she came alone. I didn't ask her anything, I was scared. I just told her to go."

While Wilma talked more about feeling awful for not helping her sister when she was in trouble, Florence tried to put the pieces together. Was Carter some kind of a relative of this man, or was the thing with the same last name just a coincidence?

Florence was also certain her stepmother had told her a slightly different story when she'd first told about her sister, Iris. Wilma had told her that Iris wanted to marry a man but her parents thought they were too young, so she left the community heartbroken. The Amish man she'd wanted to marry had married someone else and Iris fell in with a wrong crowd and got pregnant. Florence distinctly remembered it. She stared at *Mamm* and wondered which version was closer to the true story.

"Florence, did you hear anything of what I just said?"

She didn't want to upset Wilma. "I'm sorry, I didn't. I'm surprised over the letter, that's all. So, none of those things in the wooden box are my *mudder's*?"

"*Nee*. That's my *schweschder's* box."

Florence nodded. "Oh, I didn't tell you. I found three letters in a different box. One for me, one for Mark, and one for Earl. They were from my *mudder*. Our *mudder*."

"Is that right?"

"*Jah. Dat* was supposed to give them to us. He had a good memory for some things and not with others." Florence giggled.

"Anything to do with trees, apples or the harvest, he wasn't forgetful."

"I know. I'm glad we had this talk."

"Me too, Florence. We should've talked about it at the time."

"We should've." Florence figured *Mamm* might not have remembered all the details over Iris. She couldn't imagine that Wilma would've lied to her on purpose.

CHAPTER 24

THE VERY NEXT day after breakfast, Christina arrived to collect her *kapps*. She was nice and also grateful to everyone for their help, but said she couldn't stay long because she was in a rush.

The moment she left, Joy tugged on Florence's sleeve as they were walking back into the house after waving to Christina. "Can I speak to you for a moment, Florence?"

Florence loved it when her siblings singled her out to have a talk. "Of course you can." She immediately saw from Joy's pouting bottom lip that she was upset about something. "What's upset you?"

"It's Isaac."

"Really? I thought you both got along really well. Has he done something to upset you?"

"*Nee*, he hasn't done anything to upset me, it's more about him having done nothing."

"In what way?"

"I'm just not sure how he feels about me."

Florence couldn't stop smiling when she thought about Isaac's face when he was around Joy. "Everyone can see he's in love with you."

"That's what I thought too, but he's never said it."

"Does he have to say it in words? Can't he show it to you in other ways? Can't you see it in his smile? I can."

Joy sighed. "I'm not in a rush to get married like some other people we know, but I just want to know that he'll be the one I'll be marrying, later on, and at the right time."

"If you both want the same things, then, it'll happen. Don't worry so much."

"That's easy to say, but not so easy to do. I've tried not to worry about it."

"Do you have a need to hear the exact words, *I love you?*"

"I guess I do. It's not that, so much. I just want some sort of a commitment that we will be having a life with each other—together. When we first started seeing more of one another, he said things then about our future as if we'd be married and have a family, but since Honor's wedding, he hasn't said anything. I'm worried that he's not so sure about me now. He gets frustrated with me sometimes. I just thought that was normal. Everyone gets like that with me."

"I seriously think you're worried over nothing."

"It's not nothing. It's how I feel, and the thing is, I don't know what to do about it."

Florence giggled.

"What's funny?"

"It is funny that you come to me for advice. Do you see me happily married with a family?"

"*Nee*, I don't, but you are the most sensible person I know. You might have made mistakes in the past and you might do things differently now if you had the chance."

Florence raised her eyebrows. "I hope I do have another chance at love, but the sad thing is I don't know where I went wrong. As far as I knew things between me and Ezekiel were fine and then all of a sudden, he didn't want me to visit him. I've never heard from him since."

"I'm so sorry, Florence."

"It's okay. When I was about your age, I liked a

few young men but they didn't give me a second look."

"That was their loss."

"Thanks for saying that."

"I don't know why they passed you over. You would've been pretty back then when you were young."

Florence smiled at the compliment Joy was trying to give her. That described exactly how she felt —old and passed over, except when Carter was around. When she was with him, she felt like the most beautiful, loved, and cared for woman in the world.

"I know you're not that old yet. You're not as old as *Mamm,* but you're well on your way there. What advice can you give me?"

"Well, if I can give you any advice at all …" She thought about it for a moment. *"Nee,* I can't think of one piece of advice to give you. You're sensible enough to figure things out for yourself."

"I tried some hinting to make him say how he felt last night, but he didn't take any of them."

"What kind of hints?"

"I was talking about Mercy having a *boppli* and starting her family and asking him what he thought about that."

"Oh, and he didn't know you were hinting?"

"I didn't want him to know I was hinting."

"You're better at this than I am."

"Oh, Florence, I know you have the answer somewhere deep in your head. If you were to give me one piece of advice, what would it be?"

"Isaac likes his food, so why don't you keep cooking for him?" It was lame, but she knew no other advice to give her.

"I cook for him all the time and he knows I'm a good cook already."

"Why don't you take him out one day for a picnic? On a Saturday afternoon and then it will be just the two of you in a deserted field somewhere. Under a tree or by the water—somewhere you can both relax and be yourselves."

"That's a great idea. We've never been on a picnic together. And he does love his food." She leaned forward and gave Florence a kiss. "See, I knew you'd have the answer. A picnic is the answer." Joy turned and raced upstairs.

Florence wished her own problems could be solved with a picnic. All the time she was worried about her sisters marrying too young, but at least they all sought men in the Amish faith and hadn't gone looking outside the community for love.

CHAPTER 25

When Mercy went home, everyone was upset. Joy decided to concentrate on Isaac to help her get over Mercy leaving. Joy had taken Florence's advice and the next day that Isaac had a scheduled day off, they went on a picnic.

He collected her in his buggy, and when they turned onto the road, Joy tried to set a romantic mood. "Don't you just love the summer, when it's warm on a Saturday afternoon?"

"I do, when I'm not working."

"Well, you're not working today."

"*Nee*, I'm not."

She directed him to a grassy park she knew about and as they neared it, he asked, "What is the occasion of this picnic? You still haven't told me."

"Can't we just go on a nice picnic together just the two of us?"

"Sure."

"Then we can be alone and talk about things that we never get to talk about when we are surrounded by people."

He pulled up the buggy and then she ran to the back and got out the blanket and the basket.

When he had secured the horse, he came around to her.

Without her saying anything he took the basket and the blanket from her. "Where shall we go?"

"Anywhere you want."

He opened the blanket in the middle of the park. "It certainly is isolated around here."

"It's not. You're here and so that means it's not very isolated."

Once he had spread the blanket and set the basket in the middle, she sat down, opened the basket and handed him the cider with two glasses. "You pour," she ordered.

He sat down and poured out two glasses while she spread the food out.

"So, what's this all about?" He handed her a glass.

"Nothing."

He raised an eyebrow. "Are you sure?"

He was making her nervous. "I thought it would be a romantic thing to do—to go for a picnic."

"It is, I guess—but it wouldn't be if you've brought me out here to break up with me." He drank a mouthful of cider.

"No, never."

He put his hand to his heart and looked relieved, giving a little chuckle.

She gasped. "Is that what you thought?"

"*Jah*, I did. Now I can relax." He looked down at the food. "This looks great."

She passed him a plate of fried chicken and he took a piece. As he ate it, he kept looking at the rest of the food. He seemed more interested in it than in her.

Perhaps it might have been a mistake to put so much effort into the food.

"You're a good cook, Joy."

"I have been told that."

"*Jah*, by me."

"And other people."

"Are you sure you didn't bring me here to break up with me? And now you're only staying with me because you feel sorry for me?"

"Stop it. I have no intention of ever breaking up with you, don't you see that?"

"For real?"

"*Jah*. What happened to the confident Isaac that I first met?"

"That was before I liked you and now you make me nervous."

Joy giggled. "Do I?"

"You sure do."

"How do I make you nervous?"

He'd just bitten off half of the chicken meat on a drumstick, and she had to wait for him to chew and swallow his mouthful. Meanwhile, she took a sip of apple cider.

"Because you're just special, you know so much about everything. You make me want to be a better person. And I've been reading my Bible a lot more because you do. It's a good habit to get into."

"I like reading it."

"That's good."

"So where do we go from here? What do you think our future holds?"

"Good things." He finished off the rest of the chicken.

"Such as?"

"Doesn't the word tell us not to worry about

tomorrow and live for the day? Why worry about tomorrow? The lilies of the field don't worry about tomorrow and they are beautifully clothed." He looked up into the sky as a bird flew past. "And the birds of the field don't gather but they have food to eat every day."

He looked pleased with himself, but he was missing her point and she had to know if he intended to marry her one day. "But we won't be worried about tomorrow if we plan for it."

"Somethings can't be planned for. I didn't plan to stay on here when I came to Mercy's wedding and I did. I'm pleased I stayed."

There was a spark of hope. "You stayed on for me?"

"Sure, and everyone knows it too."

She recalled that Christina mentioned something like that to her. If everybody knew it, then maybe he assumed that they had a future together. But why didn't he just say it? "So, you and I have a future together?"

"Who knows what the future can bring, Joy? We will have a future together if God wills it."

There was no use. She didn't know any other way to ask him whether he intended to marry her and she wasn't going to come straight out and ask him.

She grabbed a roll, broke it in half and chomped on it trying to be satisfied with the answers he had given.

***

AFTER THE SUNDAY meeting the very next day, Joy was in her bedroom crying because Isaac didn't stay for the singing like he'd done nearly every Sunday afternoon. Neither did he come to her house. He made some excuse that he had to do something and that was all. It was so out of character for him that she was sure she'd gone too far at the picnic. She'd scared him off.

She decided to come home with Florence and *Mamm,* who never stayed for the young people's singing.

It was a shock when she looked out her bedroom window and saw his buggy at around four in the afternoon. She hurried downstairs to meet him.

When he saw her walking to the buggy, he said, "I've got a surprise for you."

"For me?" Was it flowers, at long last? "What is it?"

"Come with me."

"I can't, I've got to help with the dinner."

"We're not going anywhere."

"Oh. Where do you want me to go?"

"Stay there and close your eyes." He took her by her hand. "Keep your eyes closed."

"They are."

"Keep them closed. We're just going a couple of more steps. Stay there," he ordered as he dropped her hand.

She was so tempted to peek, but she didn't. "Why, what is it?"

"If you be quiet, you'll soon see."

"Okay, but it's not easy for me to be quiet."

"I know that much."

She laughed and stopped when she heard him open the buggy doors and then she heard some scratching noises.

"Open your eyes," he ordered.

When she opened her eyes, the first thing she saw was a ball of golden fur on the buggy floor. She let out a squeal. "He's the cutest ever." It was a small puppy.

"He's yours."

"Mine?"

"*Jah*. I even cleared it with Wilma."

"*Mamm* agreed? What? Can I keep him?"

"Of course, otherwise I wouldn't have done it. I plan to keep in good with your *mudder*."

"Can I hold him?"

"He's yours." He placed the dog in her arms and she hugged him to herself.

"I can't believe it, I just can't believe it."

"He's a boy." Isaac chuckled. "Is that better than a bunch of roses?"

"Much better, so much better. Much better and better and bestest." She giggled. "How did you know I wanted a dog of my very own?"

He laughed. "I didn't. I'm glad to hear that you do."

"Who wouldn't love a puppy? Oh, I do love him." The puppy lay there with large brown eyes looking at them both, then he put his face up to Joy's and licked her chin causing her to giggle. "I've never had a dog before. Cherish had one because she was spoiled and she got everything she wanted. Now I've got one. I just can't believe it."

"Well, you better believe it because he's yours. I'm here to spoil you now."

"*Denke* so much. This is the best thing ever. It's the best thing anyone has ever done for me. I don't know what to say. Where did you get him from?"

"I got him from the shelter. Someone found him and his brothers. They'd been dumped. There were three of them. By the time I got to the shelter, he was the last one."

"Denke."

"You can stop thanking me now." He chuckled.

"I don't think I'll ever stop thanking you, he's so adorable."

He laughed. "He is pretty cute, isn't he?"

"Sure is. When the girls get home from the singing, they won't be able to believe it." She started walking off toward the house.

"Wait up. I've got food and things for him."

She waited with him while he gathered the dog's things. He had bought food, wormer, a few toys, and a dog bed. "You thought of everything."

"They told me what he'd need, and oh, he's already had the necessary shots, and he's been neutered."

"I didn't think he'd be old enough."

"He is. He's been at the shelter awhile."

She hugged the pup. "Oh, the poor little puppy."

"Not any more. Looks like he's going to have a great home now."

"He will for sure." They walked to the house together. "I'll have to think of a good name."

CHAPTER 26

FLORENCE HAD WAITED days to work up the courage to see Carter again. Today was the day. Just when she walked out of the house, she saw a horse and buggy approaching. She'd greet the visitor and leave them with *Mamm*. That was her plan until she saw who was driving the buggy.

Ezekiel Troyer!

She walked over to him when he pulled up.

"Ezekiel, this is a surprise."

He got out of the buggy, took off his hat and held it close to his chest. "Can we talk somewhere Florence? Alone?"

She glanced over at the house. No one was about. "How about we talk on the porch?"

He slowly nodded.

"How is your family?" she asked as they walked.

"They're well."

They walked up the two wooden porch steps. "What brings you back here?"

"You bring me here, Florence. You bring me back."

She stared at him trying to take in his words, then she sat down on one of the porch chairs and he sat down on the other.

"I was a fool not to ask you to marry me the very first time I met you. I know I'll never meet another woman as good as you, Florence. You're *wunderbaar*."

Florence forced a smile, to cover the awkwardness. He was too late. Her heart belonged to Carter.

"When I heard about your secret admirer, my world felt like it was crumbling around me. If it's not too late, Florence, and you haven't given that other man your answer, I would like you to consider marrying me."

Florence's eyes bugged out. "You want me to marry you?"

"*Jah.* I'm hoping you will."

"I don't know what to say." If she married him, she would be forced to forget all about Carter, and maybe that was the answer. Ezekiel was a good man, he would look after her, care for her and be a good husband to her, and a splendid father for any *kinner* they might be blessed with.

Would it be best to turn her back on Carter to ensure her place by God's side for eternity? The other choice was an uncertain future with a man she barely knew anything about. Marriage to Ezekiel was the logical choice since they were of the same world.

It seemed *Gott* was serving her two choices on a plate.

Was this a test?

If Carter was such a bad choice, why did her heart and every fiber of her being want him so bad? Surely it would be better to live alone than to be married to someone she didn't love.

She cleared her throat. "Ezekiel, I have to be honest with you. I don't have feelings of love for you. I know you're a good man, but you deserve someone who loves you."

"Love will grow after marriage."

His words disturbed her. "Does that mean you don't love me?"

"You're a good woman and when we commit to each other in love, *Gott's* love will water our relationship with seeds of love."

Florence grimaced and stopped herself telling him that you don't water anything with seeds. "And you'd marry me knowing you don't love me and I don't love you?"

"I have feelings for you or I wouldn't have been upset when Ada told me about the other man. I hope it's not too late. Is it?"

All this was Ada's fault. She shook her head. "It's not too late. Can I have a few days to think about it?"

He bounded to his feet. "I'm leaving on Friday. I would like to have an answer before then. I can't leave my farm too long."

"Sure. I understand." She stood up. He rubbed her shoulder with one hand and then placed his hat back on his head.

Leaning on the porch railing, she watched him get into his buggy and drive his horse and buggy away. The horse was one of Samuel's, so she knew he was staying with Ada and Samuel.

When he was gone, her sisters spilled out the front door, pushing and shoving one another.

"What did he want?" asked Favor.

"Nothing, nothing much."

"We heard it, I'm sorry," Joy said. "He's got a loud voice."

"You heard it all?"

"We heard everything he said." Favor giggled. "Wait until I tell *Mamm*."

"Is that all right, Florence?" Hope asked. "*Mamm* didn't hear it."

Florence shrugged her shoulders. "Might as well I guess."

The girls ran inside looking for their mother. Florence sighed. It would've been better that they didn't know. Now she felt extra pressure to make a decision. If she married Ezekiel, the only reason to do so was to put an end to things between her and Carter. But, is that something she wanted to do?

First, she had to ask Carter a few things about himself.

She sat down on the porch chair once more. The thing that nagged in the back of her mind was that for an Amish woman of her age—in her late twenties —it was madness to let a man like Ezekiel slip through her fingers especially if she wanted *kinner*. The sensible thing to do was take him up on his offer.

"Are you going to marry him?" a small voice asked.

Florence turned to see Joy standing on the porch and hugging her puppy. "I don't know. I don't have feelings for him. I'm not in love with him."

"I understand. You can't do it then."

Florence shrugged her shoulders. "He said love would come."

Joy moved closer. "And, it might not. You might end up hating the sight of him and his pigs."

Florence burst out laughing. "I know. Love might come, but it might not."

"Besides, you can't leave the orchard, you just can't. No one else knows what to do. It'd be left to me and I wouldn't do everything as good as you can."

"We didn't even talk about whether I'd have to leave."

"Well, of course you would. He's not going to move here, is he? You've never met his family and what if you don't get along with them and you're stuck there?"

She stared at Joy. Those were all good points. "Thank you, Joy. I've got a lot of thinking to do."

"You have. Is Ezekiel coming back for dinner?"

"Not tonight."

Favor stuck her head out the front door. "Florence, *Mamm* wants to talk with you."

"This'll be good." Joy smiled at Florence.

"I might as well get this over with. I'm feeling a lecture coming on. She'll want me to marry him."

"Maybe."

Florence and Joy walked into the house and saw *Mamm,* Hope and Favor sitting in the living room.

"Come sit by me, Florence." *Mamm* patted the chair next to her.

As soon as Florence was seated, *Mamm* said, "Tell us about your proposal."

"There's not much to it."

"Is that the first time a man has ever proposed?" Hope asked.

"Jah, sadly it is."

"Sadly?" *Mamm* asked. "You've had many men interested in you and you pay them no mind."

"I don't know if that's true, but you can think that if you want."

"Are you going to marry him?" *Mamm* persisted.

"Truthfully, I don't know what to do. I'm not in love with him, and neither is he in love with me, but he'd be a good husband."

She looked up from under her eyelashes at her stepmother wondering if she had been in love with *Dat,* or whether it was a marriage of convenience for either one of them, or both.

Hope asked, "Where would you live?"

Florence looked at Hope. "I didn't even think to ask."

"You can't leave us and the orchard," *Mamm* said. "We need you."

"*Jah,* don't leave us," Favor said. "He'll have to come here."

"Yeah, but he's got a pig farm. What will he do with his pigs?" asked Joy.

"He can come here and help you farm the orchard and his brothers and his mother can run the pig farm," Hope said.

"I don't think that will work. I think his mother is in ill-health and one of his brothers left."

Mamm shook her head. "Florence, before you consider his proposal seriously you do have to find out exactly what he is proposing. Where you will live and such and so forth. And then take consideration for what will become of all of us if you up and leave. None of us have the knowledge of apples that you have. We'll have to pay a manager and that will take up all our money."

"I won't let that happen. It won't come to that." Even though it was sensible to marry him, it certainly wasn't sensible to leave her orchard. She wouldn't be living if she was without her orchard. She would be miserable.

Now she was in no mood to see Carter—she didn't want to see him when she was feeling down.

When Florence went to bed that night, just before she turned off her gaslight, she pulled out her mother's letter and read it once more.

My dearest Florence,

If you're reading this letter that means I'm no longer around. I've asked your father to give you this letter when you're an adult, the same as the letters I have for Mark and Earl.

Life is so uncertain.

Nothing is forever. I want to be there always, guiding you and your brothers, whispering in your ears. If I can't be there, pay attention to my following words and keep them in your heart.

Always be kind to others.

Try to see the other person's point of view. It's just as valid as your own.

You must follow your heart rather than your head sometimes.

Don't make my mistakes.

No matter where I am, I will always love you, your father and your brothers.

Always be there for your family.

. . .

Your loving Mamm

She switched off the light, no closer to finding out what her mother's mistakes were. It clearly had nothing to do with another man like she'd first thought. Unless the answer was that her mother hadn't been in love with her father.

Why didn't she make things clearer in her letter? Could there be a clue in the words 'follow your heart'?

She had to see Carter soon. Once she saw him again everything would become clear. She was certain of it.

CHAPTER 27

The next evening after dinner, Goldie, Joy's new pup, was in trouble for destroying two pairs of shoes and a pair of socks. Joy took him outside with her while she talked with Isaac on the porch.

"I'm just so upset that Mercy is gone. She'll have the *boppli* somewhere else and I won't see it until it's probably a-year-old or something."

"Don't be sad. How about we see if we can go up there somehow and see her sooner, when the baby is born. Or when it's a few weeks old we'll go up. Wilma probably won't let us go alone, so what if I take all of you there?"

Joy giggled. "You'd do that?"

"If it would keep that beautiful smile on your face I'd do anything."

"Sounds like you love me." She put Goldie down and he sat by her feet.

"I do. With all my heart."

"You do?"

"Of course. I thought you'd know that."

"You've never said so."

"I didn't know I would have to." He sat down on the porch to pat the pup.

She sat down on the boards of the porch, on the other side of Goldie. "Isaac, would you marry me?"

"Yes, of course we'll get married." He continued to stroke Goldie.

"We will?"

"There's no one else for me, Joy, and there never will be. I'm sorry if I never made that clear to you. I don't know what I'd do without you. I need to see you every day."

She nodded. "I feel the same."

"When do you want to get married?"

"I don't know, I don't care. As long as I know that you want to marry me, that's all I care about."

"I've saved up some money, so when I've got enough to support us both, along with Goldie, let's get married."

"I've got money too. We can put it together and then we'll have double."

He laughed. "Whatever makes you happy, Joy. That's all I've ever wanted."

"Me too." She leaned across Goldie and put her arms around him and hugged him tight.

CHAPTER 28

SHE HOPED he wasn't upset with her for not stopping by sooner. She hadn't been ready to talk to him then, but now she *had* to see him. She walked through the orchard with her heart racing. She was sure she heard the sounds of a buggy pulling up to the house and was pleased. Visitors meant that everybody would be occupied and no one would notice she was missing. She kept going.

When she saw Carter's house, she noticed his car and that told her he was home.

Just as she was making her way through the fence, he came out of the front door. He must have seen her. She was halfway through the fence when the ties of her apron snagged on the upper row of barbed wire.

She turned around to unhook herself and that was when she saw Ezekiel. That must've been Ezekiel's buggy that she had heard.

This wasn't good. She wanted to yell at him to go back to the house and she'd see him soon but she couldn't. She glanced over her other shoulder and saw Carter making his way toward her.

Her two possible futures were about to collide.

Carter had his eyes so fixed on her, he didn't see anyone else. "I'm so glad you've finally come. There are some things you need to know about me."

Ezekiel had the worst timing in the world. She looked over at Ezekiel and then looked back at Carter.

It was then that Carter noticed they had company. "What I've got to say will have to wait."

"I'm sorry."

He nodded, and said quietly, "Me too."

She wasn't sure what to do, but with her apron securely snagged on the fence, she wasn't going anywhere quickly.

Carter busied himself helping to free her.

"Just rip it," she said about her apron.

"You sure?"

"Yes."

Ezekiel reached them just as she was freed and

now Florence was on the opposite side of the fence to Ezekiel, standing next to Carter.

"Hello," Ezekiel said staring at Carter.

"Oh, Ezekiel, you haven't met Carter yet, have you?"

"No, I haven't."

"Ezekiel Troyer, meet Carter Braithwaite."

"Nice to meet you." Carter walked forward and held out his hand. Ezekiel stepped forward and shook it. Then, Ezekiel just stood there and Florence knew she would have to say something, but Carter spoke again. "Florence, you've finally come to approve those renovations, have you?"

He was giving her an excuse, but it did sound fake. "That's right." She looked over at Ezekiel. "I'm sorry, I didn't know you were coming to dinner tonight."

"Your mother invited me. I told you I was only here for a few days."

"Yes, I know that." She looked around nervously at Carter.

"I see what's going on here." Ezekiel glared at the two of them. "I shouldn't have returned for you, Florence. I made a big mistake, and now I know why you stopped writing."

He turned and strode away. She was tempted to

point out that she only stopped writing because of the tone of his last letter, which practically—pretty thoroughly, really—told her they had no future.

As she watched Ezekiel go, she couldn't find a place within her that cared; not her heart or her mind, and even her good manners were letting her down at this point.

There was nothing she could say; it was best to let him walk away.

Then she was worried that Carter might think that she liked Ezekiel. She turned back to him. "There's nothing between him and me."

He smirked. "I know."

"How could you?"

"What we have is rare and special. You're the once-in-a-lifetime love for me, Florence. Come away with me?"

If only she could. She was so lost in his unusual colored eyes, she asked, "Where to?"

"Anywhere."

"Okay. No, wait. The orchard."

"What's keeping you from being with me? Is it the orchard, or your faith?"

"My faith. We can't be—I can't be tied with an unbeliever."

"I believe."

"Do you?"

"Yes. I believe in you, I believe in me, and I believe in our love. The first time I saw you, I knew you were special. You were in a buggy driving, and your sisters were in the back. There was something about you, that face, the slight apprehension across your brow. I knew then the type of person you were. I could tell."

"You mean you saw me before your cows broke through the fence that day?"

A wide smile revealed his perfect teeth. "I did."

She licked her lips. "Why don't you learn about us and our ways?"

"I only desire you. Marry me and do what you want. Believe in what you want and I will respect that. I'm offering you marriage and all of myself. I know with your faith you probably wouldn't feel right about living with a man, so I'm offering you everything I am."

She sighed. Her thrill from him loving her was entangled within the reasons they couldn't be together. "If only things were that simple."

"What do you want, Florence?"

"What I'd like is you and to still have my family and be in the community with you in the community as well."

"I can give myself to you, but with me—"

"Stop!" She put her hands over her ears not wanting to hear words that would shatter her dreams. Why couldn't she have it all? Surely God would make a way for them to be together.

He moved in and gently pulled her hands away from her ears. "I do believe in God, but I can't have an organized religion telling me how to live my life."

If she got away and prayed really, really hard, God might work on his heart. "It's not like that. We *want* to do what we do."

He pulled her in towards him for a hug and they embraced. "I'll give you time," he whispered. "I'm not going anywhere."

"And I'll give *you* time."

He laughed and then she laughed, but only because she felt so good to be in his arms.

"Oh Florence, It would be cruel if we didn't end up together. I don't know who that man was just now, but he's not for you. The only man for you is me."

She pulled away slightly and looked into his eyes. She knew that was true. It had to be him or nobody; she'd never settle for second best. "Thank you."

He laughed. "Why are you thanking me?"

She shrugged. "I just am. I have to go."

"Don't! I wake up every day hoping you'll stop by. It's hard for me as a man not to have control over my destiny. I can't call you, I can't text you, I can't stop by and see you. I wait here hoping I'll see you through that window." He pointed back at his house.

"I'll come back tomorrow."

"Do you promise?"

"I said it, so that's as good as a promise."

He shook his head. "I've heard it before, though, and you didn't come back."

"I'm sorry. I will this time." She shook her head, having nothing else to say.

He took hold of her hand and squeezed it. "I'll be here waiting all day."

They smiled at each other, and then she said, "Help me with the fence?"

"Sure." He pulled the wires of the fence apart for her to slip through. "I'll see you tomorrow, Florence Baker."

"See you tomorrow, Carter Braithwaite." She walked back through the orchard with a song in her heart and music in every fiber of her being, as the fresh afternoon breeze tickled her cheeks.

The wind swept through the stray hairs flying free of her prayer *kapp*, and she realized today had been the best day of her life. He loved her and she loved him. What's more, he wanted to marry her.

The only thing she wasn't happy about was that she still hadn't asked Carter questions.

How could she leave the Amish for a man she knew nothing about just because he made her happy? She had to know what made him the man that he was—his history, his present, and what he desired for his future.

Tomorrow ... tomorrow, she had to ask him some serious questions and not be distracted by wanting to touch him and be in his arms.

She had to get those answers.

The closer she got to her house, the sadder she became. She was away from Carter and the secret world she'd built up in her mind—back to reality.

She was relieved when she saw no buggy. *Mamm* came out of the house to meet her.

"Ezekiel was very upset."

"Oh, that's too bad. Did he go into the *haus?*"

"*Jah*, and he said that you were flirting with the man next door."

Florence's mouth fell open. "I wasn't."

"He was so upset that he took the buggy, leaving Samuel and Ada here."

"Oh no, really?"

"Jah. They're hoping one of the girls will take them home later after dinner. I'll have Joy do it."

Florence nodded.

"Samuel saw how upset he was and told him he could take the buggy. I think it's best to keep you away from Ezekiel for a while."

"I didn't mean to upset him, truly I didn't. I don't even know why he got so upset. All I was doing was talking to the man next door. I got snagged in the fence and they both came over to help me out and then I introduced the two of them." Florence lifted up her apron to show her the small hole where it had gotten snagged.

"Is that all that happened?"

"That's all."

"You weren't flirting with the man next door?"

"Mamm, I wouldn't know how to flirt. I couldn't do it if I tried."

"That's not good. Misunderstandings are so bad. Like the one you and I had over the letter. You should explain yourself to him."

"Nee, Mamm. I don't want Ezekiel as my husband."

"This is the first time I've heard that."

"I don't think he's treated me very well. He treated me like a child just now and embarrassed me in front of our neighbor and now he's come back and told everyone things that aren't true. Not to mention how he canceled my visit when I was trying to give him a chance. I haven't forgotten about that, and he never apologized. He'll never be my husband."

Wilma put her arm around Florence's waist. "Love is hard sometimes, but we must battle through it."

"Well I'll do that battling with somebody else, not with him."

Mamm nodded. "Okay. I'll tell Ada later."

"*Denke.*"

"Don't get upset." She patted Florence on the arm.

"I'll try not to."

∼

During dinner, it was evident that Florence had upset both Ada and Samuel. Samuel wouldn't even look at her.

In the middle of dinner, Favor said, "Ezekiel said you were flirting, Florence."

"Shush, Favor," Joy said.

"Well that's what I heard him say. I didn't know it was a secret. Everyone knows."

"Why talk about it, then?" *Mamm* glared at Favor.

"Because I have an idea. I hope you'll like it. We send Florence to Aunt Dagmar and get Cherish back."

Florence looked down into her food, embarrassed, while Hope dug Favor in the ribs. "Ow! That hurt."

"Stop saying mean things."

"I'm not. Everyone's been quiet and everyone's upset with Florence. Everyone is thinking, *who is this man next door and why haven't we met him?*"

"Honor's met him because he's the one who drove all that way to bring her back … that time." Florence didn't want to remind everyone that Honor had run away with Jonathon.

"And that was a complete waste of time because they ended up getting married anyway—Honor and Jonathon. You should've just let them run away."

Joy shook her head. *"Nee.* Now they're in the community; if they'd stayed away, they wouldn't have been, silly."

"Now girls, let's just have a nice quiet dinner, shall we?" Ada asked.

Florence noticed that *Mamm* was quiet and just looked sad. Was she looking that way because she missed *Dat?*

CHAPTER 29

When everyone had finished the dessert, Florence and some of the other girls cleared the table and suddenly Florence found herself alone in the kitchen with Ada.

"I hope you're not upset with me, Ada." Florence knew Ada was upset because she wasn't doing a very good job of hiding it.

"I think you've made a big mistake about Ezekiel."

"I tried. I did try."

"I'm not sure you did. It seems like you've known that man next door for quite a while. Ezekiel never had a chance."

Florence turned on the water for the dishes.

"Did he?" Ada persisted.

"He had a chance. I was giving him a chance."

"I suppose you were in your own way. Tell me this, how much of your heart was in it?"

"Not much, if I'm honest. I just wasn't feeling much for him. He was nice, but sort of like a friend."

"You don't make these decisions by feeling it."

She turned around and stared at Ada. "You don't?"

"When I first met Samuel, I didn't like him at all."

Florence giggled and wondered if she was exaggerating. "That's hard to believe you get on so well together."

"Only because of the hard years of marriage behind us. My *mudder* thought he would be good for me and she was right. She was the one who pushed us together. Her and Samuel's dear *mudder,* bless her heart."

"I'm sure that's not the case for everybody. I'm sure people have made the same decisions and things didn't end up well for them."

"Florence, look how old you are; you're not going to get many more opportunities. There aren't many single men around your age or close to it. All the widowers are a lot older than you."

Florence nodded. "I'm not worried about it at all."

"If you want to get married, you should be worried. You should be praying."

"Maybe I don't want to get married."

"You can't be serious."

"I have everything I want right here. Why would I need to change anything?" It wasn't true. She did want true love and companionship.

"You think your life's so good here?"

Florence nodded. "I'm not complaining."

"What if Wilma wanted to get married again?"

The idea didn't sit well with Florence, unless that meant she'd get to live alone in the house. "There's nothing stopping her from doing so. She can do what she wants."

"I think there is. What if you were standing in her way?"

"I'd never—"

Joy walked into the kitchen. "Excuse me, but Isaac and I have an announcement to make."

Ada smiled "I hope it's what I think it might be."

"Take a seat and find out."

Florence wiped her hands on the hand towel and followed Ada out of the kitchen. Joy pulled her aside. "Don't worry, Florence. I knew Ezekiel wasn't for you. He was nice and everything, but you need someone extra special."

"*Denke*, Joy."

"You deserve to be happy."

"*Denke.*"

Florence sat on the couch next to *Mamm*, and then Joy and Isaac stood in the middle of the room. They exchanged beaming smiles, and then Isaac looked around at everyone as he cleared his throat. He took hold of Joy's hand. "We're getting married."

Wilma let out a squeal and hurried over to hug them. Everyone was delighted. Joy laughed. "I didn't know he was going to blurt it out like that."

Ada didn't seem surprised. "Have you spoken to the bishop about when this wedding will be?"

"Not for a while," Joy said once her mother let her go.

"We've decided on a long engagement to give us time to save up a little," Isaac told them.

Joy said, "I don't want to move into Mark and Christina's *haus*."

"It's so small it would be a little crowded," Isaac added.

Wilma nodded. "That's right it would."

"You sat there all throughout dinner keeping this to yourselves?" Samuel asked, grinning.

"That's right. We weren't sure when to tell everyone. Then we thought it was the right time." Isaac looked at Joy for approval and she gave a nod.

"When did he ask you to marry him, Joy?" Favor asked.

Joy glanced at Isaac. "Only very recently." She smiled at Isaac. No one needed to know that she was the one who had asked him. He would've asked her in time.

Meanwhile, Florence was pleased that the focus was off her. "Congratulations to both of you." She hugged Isaac and then Joy.

"I made some chocolate cake earlier," Favor said. "Why don't we have some of that now?"

"Good idea," said Hope. "I'll help you get it."

Samuel still didn't have much to say to Florence and she didn't know why he was so upset. He didn't even seem pleased for Joy and Isaac. Perhaps it was because Ada was upset with her and he was being supportive of his wife.

Ada and Samuel didn't stay long after that. After all, Ezekiel was staying at their house and they had to get back to him. Isaac drove them home before he went back to Mark and Christina's place.

Florence went to bed that night pleased that Joy had chosen that moment to make her announcement. After she had, no one mentioned the man next door again or her supposed flirting.

She moved to the window and sat on the floor looking up into the night sky. Carter was only a few hundred yards away.

What would her life be like if she left it all behind for him? Would she marry him and live in his house and still run the orchard?

Just as she was thinking of all the possibilities, a bright star streaked across the sky. It was a shooting star—a promise of hope. Even more so because this was the first she'd ever seen.

CHAPTER 30

After breakfast the next morning, Florence just plain *had* to see Carter. She told everyone she was going for a walk and then left the house before anyone could say anything.

With the wind rushing against her face, she strode determinedly along the rows of apple trees until his house came into view.

It didn't take long before he rushed out to meet her. She hadn't even reached the fence. "You came back."

Florence put her fingers on the top row of barbed wire along the fence line. "I said I would."

"I'm pleased." He helped her through the fence by stretching apart the wires.

Then she faced him squarely and had to get her

answers. "Who are you, why did you buy the place here, and what do you do for a living?"

His face drained of color. "Are you sure you haven't left anything out?"

"I have. Are you any relation to Gerald Braithwaite?"

He blew out a deep breath. "Come inside and sit down. I'll answer all your questions." He gestured toward the house and she started walking, glad she was finally going to learn his secrets.

The house was still relatively bare, she noticed, as she made her way to one of the two couches. She sat on one and expected him to sit on the one opposite. He sat beside her.

He shook his head. "I'm not sure where to start."

"Start by telling me why you bought this place."

He nodded. "Recently, my mother died."

"Oh, I'm so sorry."

"Thank you. It wasn't that recently. It was about four years ago. It just seems like last week. Her name was Iris Braithwaite."

A cold shiver ran through Florence's entire body. Two names she knew well. Iris and Braithwaite. Iris was her stepmother's estranged sister's name. "Iris?"

"Yes. Your stepmother's sister."

She covered her mouth as she tried to put the pieces of the puzzle together in her head.

"My mother died heartbroken about her sister's rejection. She even talked about it on the day she died."

"Oh, that's so sad. Your mother was Iris, Wilma's sister, yes?"

He nodded.

"I just can't believe it. She married Gerald Braithwaite, the man who wrote that letter?"

"She did."

"I thought that letter was written to ...." She'd thought that letter from Gerald had been written to her mother before she'd married her father. "You're Gerald's son?"

"I am."

She stared at the man in disbelief. "I'm glad I'm sitting down." Now she knew she didn't have the whole truth from Wilma. "Please tell me about Iris and Gerald." She knew Carter would tell her what was what.

"You mentioned that Gerald wrote your mother a letter—"

"I know. I found out later, that letter was written to Iris."

He nodded. "Yes, I thought you had things wrong."

"There was no name mentioned on the letter and it was among my mother's things so I assumed the letter was hers." She was pleased the letter hadn't been to her mother. In her heart, she wanted to keep the romantic view of her parents' relationship. "What happened to Gerald?"

"He died when I was ten."

"Oh, I'm so sorry."

He slowly nodded. "It's been tough without him. He was everything to me. We were so close."

"When did Iris and Gerald marry?"

"The whole story, as she told me, went like this: she was supposed to marry some Amish man and she wasn't in love with him, she was in love with Gerald. They'd been having a secret relationship for six months before she left the Amish to be with him. The thing was, my father wasn't yet divorced from his first wife—separated but not divorced."

"Oh."

"It gets worse. Dad hadn't told her that he was still married and my mother wasn't happy. She found out just weeks after she left the community. He'd promised her marriage and then she expected it right away. He told her why there had to be a delay."

"Oh, she wouldn't have liked that."

"You're right. She didn't. They had a huge fight and split up. My mother found out she was pregnant soon after the break-up and didn't tell him. He went up north and she battled on for a while by herself and had the child—me. When I was around six months old, she called him in desperate need for money just to feed me. She told him about me and by that time he was divorced, and they got back together."

"That's good. Finally. Were they happy together?"

He smiled. "Very."

She placed both hands over her chest. "I'm so pleased for them. Wilma said Iris came to the door one day and she turned her away. Wilma regretted it ever since."

"Mom went through some hard times. I know that much."

"Why did you buy the farm here? You must've known at the time that Wilma was right there, next door."

He ran his hand over his cropped dark hair. "I knew. You might not understand this, so I'll just say it the best I can. It feels a little bit like I'm home knowing my mother's sister is next door, and there's a certain comfort in knowing I'm in the same vicinity where my mother was raised."

It made perfect sense. He wasn't that different from her. That was why she loved the orchard so much; it reminded her of her parents and she felt close to them and comforted.

"I know it's silly, but it's the truth."

"I believe you." She stared at him trying to see a family resemblance. "You don't look much like my stepmother."

He laughed. "She's my aunt. I can tell you that I was relieved when I learned you were Wilma's stepdaughter, otherwise we would've been cousins."

She rubbed her forehead. It all felt like a weird dream. Also, she wasn't sure the timeline of Wilma's story matched. She was certain Wilma told her she turned her sister away when Mercy was a baby. The truth would come out eventually. "What are your plans? Will you tell Wilma?"

"I don't think so. It's best to leave the past in the past."

"Yes, but you're here now. You're in the present and she'd be so pleased to know you."

"I don't know about that." He reached out and took hold of her hand. "Now that you know everything, where do we go from here?"

She was so tempted to say she'd go to the end of the world with him and back again. Still, there were so many things she didn't know. "What do you do for work?"

"I have a company that designs games."

"What kind of games?"

"Ones that you'd use on a phone, or a computer. My chess app for instance is one of my games."

"I kind of understand. That gives you a living?"

His lips turned upward just slightly. "I manage okay."

"That's good. Now that I know everything, I don't know why you didn't just tell me." She held her head.

"What do you think now that you know? Does it make a difference to how you feel about me?"

"It shows me how far apart we are in everything that we believe."

He placed his other hand over the top of hers. "That'll make life interesting."

"Or tear us apart."

"Never. I'll respect you enough to know you'll have your own opinion on things and I'll never try to change you."

She stared at him not being able to say the same. Their lives were so different. It wasn't that they had differing opinions of things. It wasn't that simple. Summoning all her strength, she withdrew her hand and stood up. "I'll have to think about everything you've just told me. It's a lot to take in at once."

He stood up and placed his hands lightly on her shoulders. "Don't leave me, Florence. I don't want to spend another day wondering what's in our future. I want us to be together, and that's why I asked you to marry me."

She was relieved he was serious about her. If only he were an Amish man. Why was life so challenging? "I've got lots to consider."

"Like what?"

"There's the orchard. If I'm with you, my family might turn their backs on me if I leave the community."

"I'll buy you ten more orchards. We can start our own family. All we need is each other."

She bit her lip wondering what her life would be like if she turned her back on everyone. How would Wilma cope with the girls, and everything else? They all relied on her. "I need time. I'm sorry." She walked away and grabbed the front door handle.

"Florence, if you walk away from me now, I'm going to sell out and move away."

She spun around to face him. "No! Just give me

time. That's all I'm asking. Time to think on how this will work."

He stepped closer. "This is ripping me apart. Every day without you is an eternity. I'm not going to let more years pass, hoping."

"I can't think that quickly. Just give me—"

"No! Days will turn into weeks, weeks into months and then before we know it, years would've gone by."

"But you said you want to live here to be near family."

"It's too hard for me. Come with me, Florence. Choose me! Choose me now—today!"

He walked toward her and she desperately wanted to run into his arms and tell him *yes*.

She had Wilma, she had responsibilities. If she left, she might never be welcome at home—never see Mercy's baby or any of her step-sisters' or her brothers' future children. "I can't." She turned and ran from him. Somehow, she got through the wire fence without the usual trouble, and then she kept running until she got to the first row of trees.

With her heart racing and sweat beading on her forehead, she leaned against a tree. Her mind swirled with choices while she became filled with the fear of making the wrong one.

With Carter, she could have her own family and a future. They could start their own orchard, their very own.

Back at the house, she was nothing more than a caretaker of others—the extended family of her father.

Her mother's letter jumped into her mind. *Choose with your heart, sometimes.* This was one of those times, but she was Amish. How could she choose to marry an outsider? It was against everything she'd been raised to believe.

Looking at her beautiful trees, she didn't want to leave them behind, but neither could she live with herself if she lost the only man she'd ever loved. It was a huge thing to leave the community but she'd never been baptized; technically, she wasn't a full member yet. She'd become one of the people she'd looked down upon—the people who'd left the community for love. Her heart opened to them. Now she knew how harsh her judgment of them had been.

Leading with her heart, she hurried back to Carter longing to be in his arms. Now she'd made her decision, it felt good.

She was surprised to see him at the fence line

between their two properties. He had his head down looking at something.

He looked up at her. "I'm stuck," he called out.

She walked over, smiling. "What were you doing?"

"Coming to get you."

"You were?" She giggled at him while her heart bubbled over with joy. She'd made the right choice.

"Yes. I'm not taking *no* for an answer, just as soon as I get unstuck from here." He raised his hands in the air.

She covered her mouth with her fingertips and giggled again. "I can't believe you were coming to get me."

While she walked closer, he managed to set himself free, and then he stepped through to her side of the fence. "Wait. You've come back, does that mean …"

She nodded.

"You'll marry me?" he asked.

"I will, Carter Braithwaite, son of Iris, my step-aunt, and son of Gerald Braithwaite."

He laughed, picked her up and spun her around in a circle with her long dress flying in the breeze. In that moment, she closed her eyes and knew she'd have happiness always.

He set her down on her feet and held both of her hands. "You've made a sacrifice and I know it was a hard decision. I'll make it up to you in every possible way I can."

She was too overwhelmed to speak. There were so many questions about how they'd work everything out and what would happen. Now that they'd made that full commitment to one another she'd stick to it with no turning back, no matter what. All she had to do now was break the news to her family.

They'd be shocked—really shocked. And Ada would be horrified. Ezekiel would be justified. Her step-sisters might be secretly pleased for her. Wilma would be overwhelmed with taking over so many tasks.

But, this was her life to live and this time she was going to put herself and Carter first.

"I love you, Florence Baker."

She opened her mouth in shock. "You do?"

For his answer, he lowered his mouth to hers and they shared their first proper kiss.

Thank you for reading Amish Joy.
I do hope you are enjoying the series.
Samantha Price

Book 5
Amish Family Secrets

LIES HAVE BEEN TOLD.

Secrets have been kept.

What will Florence do when she learns the truth that her stepmother has been keeping from her for many years?

Will this change Florence's plans?

~

Other books in the series:

Book 1.

Amish Mercy

Book 2.

Amish Honor

Book 3.

A Simple Kiss

For more Samantha Price books, visit: www.SamanthaPrice Author.com

OTHER BOOKS BY SAMANTHA PRICE:

AMISH MAIDS TRILOGY

Book 1 His Amish Nanny

Book 2 The Amish Maid's Sweetheart

Book 3 The Amish Deacon's Daughter

ETTIE SMITH AMISH MYSTERIES

Book 1 Secrets Come Home

Book 2 Amish Murder

Book 3 Murder in the Amish Bakery

Book 4 Amish Murder Too Close

Book 5 Amish Quilt Shop Mystery

Book 6 Amish Baby Mystery

Book 7 Betrayed

Book 8: Amish False Witness

Book 9: Amish Barn Murders

Book 10 Amish Christmas Mystery

Book 11 Who Killed Uncle Alfie?

Book 12 Lost: Amish Mystery

Book 13 Amish Cover-Up

Book 14 Amish Crossword Murder

Book 15 Old Promises

Book 16 Amish Mystery at Rose Cottage

Book 17 Amish Mystery: Plain Secrets

Book 18 Amish Mystery: Fear Thy Neighbor

AMISH MISFTIS

Book 1 The Amish Girl Who Never Belonged

Book 2 The Amish Spinster

Book 3 The Amish Bishop's Daughter

Book 4 The Amish Single Mother

Book 5 The Temporary Amish Nanny

Book 6 Jeremiah's Daughter

Book 7 My Brother's Keeper

AMISH LOVE BLOOMS

Book 1 Amish Rose

Book 2 Amish Tulip

Book 3 Amish Daisy

Book 4 Amish Lily

Book 5 Amish Violet

Book 6 Amish Willow

SEVEN AMISH BACHELORS

Book 1 The Amish Bachelor

Book 2 His Amish Romance

Book 3 Joshua's Choice

Book 4 Forbidden Amish Romance

Book 5 The Quiet Amish Bachelor

Book 6 The Determined Amish Bachelor

Book 7 Amish Bachelor's Secret

EXPECTANT AMISH WIDOWS

Book 1 Amish Widow's Hope

Book 2 The Pregnant Amish Widow

Book 3 Amish Widow's Faith

Book 4 Their Son's Amish Baby

Book 5 Amish Widow's Proposal

Book 6 The Pregnant Amish Nanny

Book 7 A Pregnant Widow's Amish Vacation

Book 8 The Amish Firefighter's Widow

Book 9 Amish Widow's Secret

Book 10 The Middle-Aged Amish Widow

Book 11 Amish Widow's Escape

Book 12 Amish Widow's Christmas

Book 13 Amish Widow's New Hope

Book 14 Amish Widow's Story

Book 15 Amish Widow's Decision

Book 16 Amish Widow's Trust

Book 17 The Amish Potato Farmer's Widow

AMISH ROMANCE SECRETS

Book 1 A Simple Choice

Book 2 Annie's Faith

Book 3 A Small Secret

Book 4 Ephraim's Chance

Book 5 A Second Chance

Book 6 Choosing Amish

AMISH WEDDING SEASON

Book 1 Impossible Love

Book 2 Love at First

Book 3 Faith's Love

Book 4 The Trials of Mrs. Fisher

Book 5 A Simple Change

AMISH BABY COLLECTION

Book 1 The Gambler's Amish Baby

Book 2 The Promise

Book 3 Abandoned

Book 4 Amish Baby Surprise

Book 5 Amish Baby Gift

Book 6 Amish Christmas Baby Gone

AMISH TWIN HEARTS

Book 1 Amish Trading Places

Book 2 Amish Truth Be Told

Book 3 The Big Beautiful Amish Woman

Book 4 The Amish Widow and The Millionaire

For more books by Samantha Price, check her website:

www.samanthapriceauthor.com

ABOUT SAMANTHA PRICE

A prolific author of Amish fiction, Samantha Price wrote stories from a young age, but it wasn't until later in life that she took up writing full time. Formally an artist, she exchanged her paintbrush for the computer and, many best-selling book series later, has never looked back.

Samantha is happiest on her computer lost in the world of her characters.

To date, Samantha has received several All Stars Awards; Harlequin has published her Amish Love Blooms series, and Amazon Studios have produced several of her books in audio.

Samantha is best known for the Ettie Smith Amish Mysteries series and the Expectant Amish Widows series.

To learn more about Samantha Price and her books visit:

www.samanthapriceauthor.com

Samantha loves to hear from her readers. Connect with her at:

samanthaprice333@gmail.com

www.facebook.com/SamanthaPriceAuthor

Follow Samantha Price on BookBub

Twitter @ AmishRomance

Made in the USA
San Bernardino, CA
23 April 2020